BILLY BATSON
AND THE MAGIC OF
SHAZAM!

STONE ARCH BOOKS
a capstone imprint

THE WEATHERMAN CALLED FOR A LITTLE LIGHTNING... SHAZAM!

▼▼ STONE ARCH BOOKS™

Published in 2014
A Capstone Imprint
1710 Roe Crest Drive
North Mankato, MN 56003
www.capstonepub.com

Originally published by DC Comics in the U.S. in single
magazine form as Billy Batson and the Magic of
SHAZAM! #3.
Copyright © 2014 DC Comics. All Rights Reserved.

DC COMICS
1700 Broadway, New York, NY 10019
A Warner Bros. Entertainment Company
No part of this publication may be reproduced in whole
or in part, or stored in a retrieval system, or transmitted
in any form or by any means, electronic, mechanical,
photocopying, recording, or otherwise, without written
permission.

Printed in China.
032014   008085LEOF14

Cataloging-in-Publication Data is available at the Library
of Congress website:
ISBN: 978-1-4342-9227-8 (library binding)

Summary: Billy Batson just wants to stay Captain
Marvel all the time and not change back into his
normal, 11-year-old self. That is, until Mary reminds
him of a problem--he has detention at school. To make
matters worse, Theo Adam kidnaps Billy in hopes of
stealing his power-granting magic word! Will Billy be
able to escape Theo, attend detention, and get his
superhero self under control?

STONE ARCH BOOKS

Ashley C. Andersen Zantop **Publisher**
Michael Dahl **Editorial Director**
Sean Tulien **Editor**
Heather Kindseth **Creative Director**
Kristi Carlson **Designer**

DC COMICS

Jann Jones Original U.S. Editor

BILLY BATSON AND THE MAGIC OF SHAZAM!

PERILOUS PERIL!

Mike Kunkel .... writer & artist

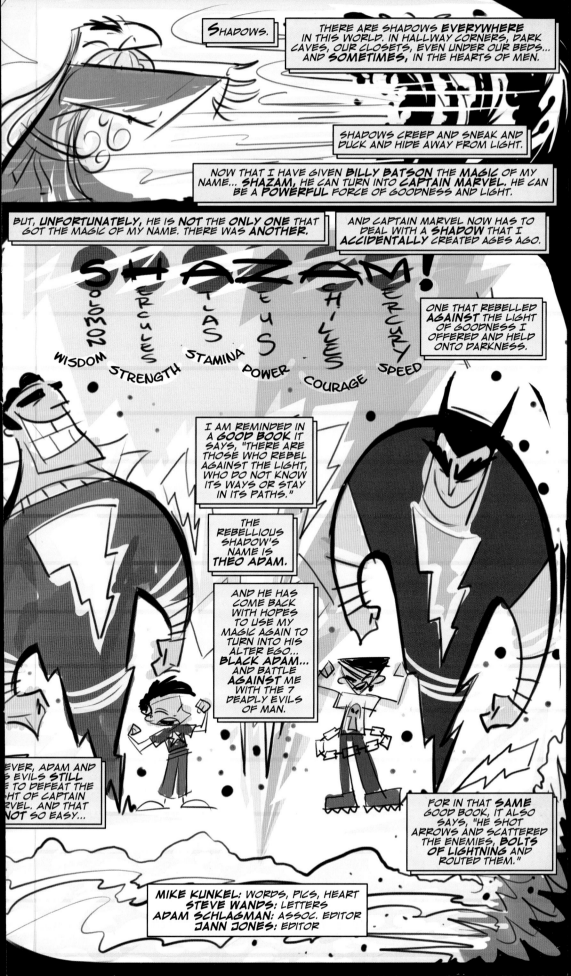

SHADOWS.

THERE ARE SHADOWS **EVERYWHERE** IN THIS WORLD. IN HALLWAY CORNERS, DARK CAVES, OUR CLOSETS, EVEN UNDER OUR BEDS... AND **SOMETIMES**, IN THE HEARTS OF MEN.

SHADOWS CREEP AND SNEAK AND DUCK AND HIDE AWAY FROM LIGHT.

NOW THAT I HAVE GIVEN **BILLY BATSON** THE **MAGIC** OF MY NAME... SHAZAM, HE CAN TURN INTO **CAPTAIN MARVEL**. HE CAN BE A **POWERFUL** FORCE OF GOODNESS AND LIGHT.

BUT, **UNFORTUNATELY**, HE IS **NOT THE ONLY ONE** THAT GOT THE MAGIC OF MY NAME. THERE WAS **ANOTHER**.

AND CAPTAIN MARVEL NOW HAS TO DEAL WITH A **SHADOW** THAT I **ACCIDENTALLY** CREATED AGES AGO.

SHAZAM!

SOLOMON
HERCULES
ATLAS
ZEUS
ACHILLES
MERCURY

WISDOM   STRENGTH   STAMINA   POWER   COURAGE   SPEED

ONE THAT REBELLED **AGAINST** THE LIGHT OF GOODNESS I OFFERED AND HELD ONTO DARKNESS.

I AM REMINDED IN A **GOOD BOOK** IT SAYS, "THERE ARE THOSE WHO REBEL AGAINST THE LIGHT, WHO DO NOT KNOW ITS WAYS OR STAY IN ITS PATHS."

THE REBELLIOUS SHADOW'S NAME IS **THEO ADAM**.

AND HE HAS COME BACK WITH HOPES TO USE MY MAGIC AGAIN TO TURN INTO HIS ALTER EGO... **BLACK ADAM**... AND BATTLE **AGAINST** ME WITH THE 7 DEADLY EVILS OF MAN.

...EVER, ADAM AND ...S EVILS **STILL** ...E TO DEFEAT THE ...HT OF CAPTAIN ...RVEL. AND THAT ...NOT SO EASY...

FOR IN THAT **SAME** GOOD BOOK, IT ALSO SAYS, "HE SHOT ARROWS AND SCATTERED THE ENEMIES, **BOLTS OF LIGHTNING** AND ROUTED THEM."

MIKE KUNKEL: WORDS, PICS, HEART
STEVE WANDS: LETTERS
ADAM SCHLAGMAN: ASSOC. EDITOR
JANN JONES: EDITOR

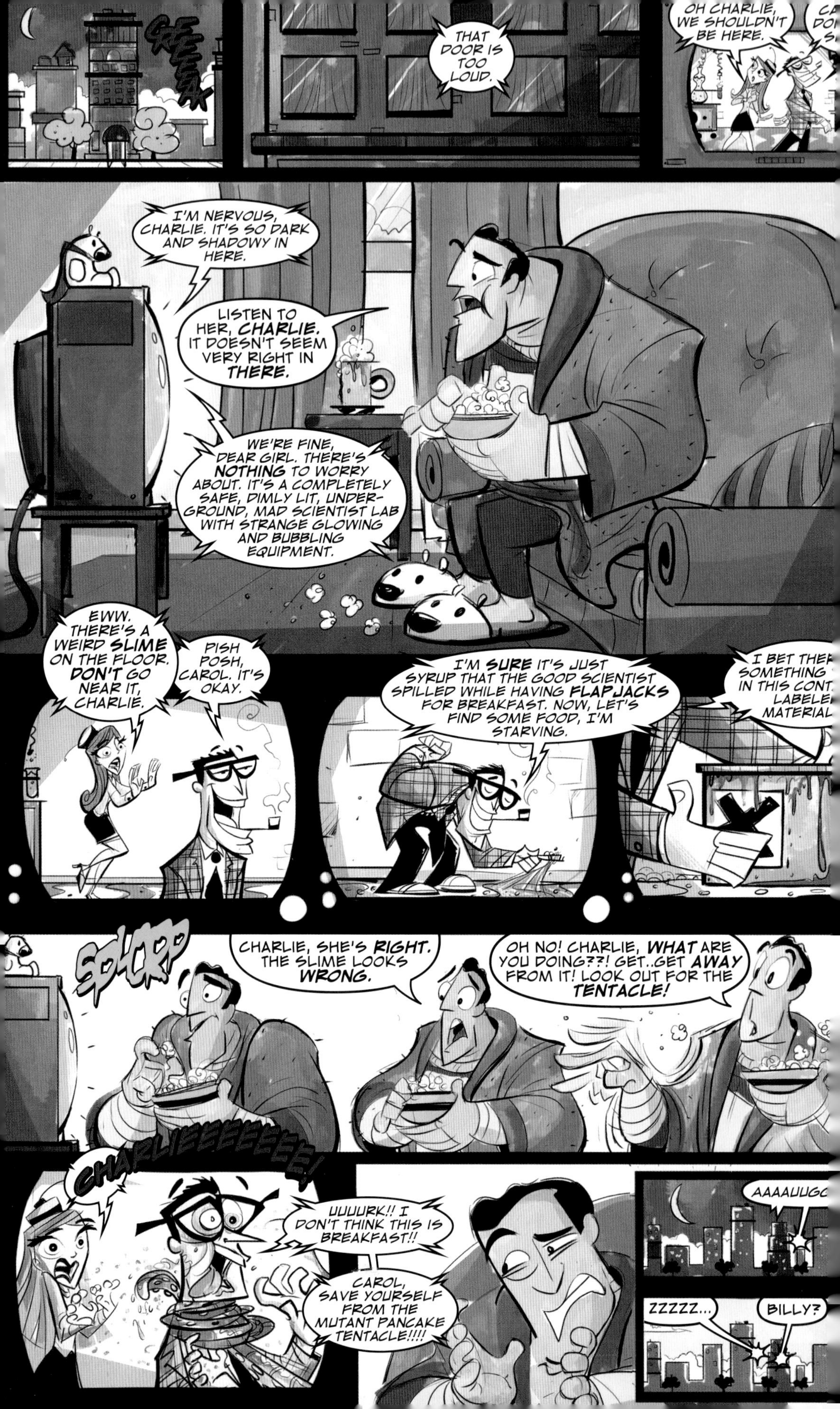

CREEEAK
THAT DOOR IS TOO LOUD.
OH CHARLIE, WE SHOULDN'T BE HERE.
I'M NERVOUS, CHARLIE. IT'S SO DARK AND SHADOWY IN HERE.
LISTEN TO HER, CHARLIE. IT DOESN'T SEEM VERY RIGHT IN THERE.
WE'RE FINE, DEAR GIRL. THERE'S NOTHING TO WORRY ABOUT. IT'S A COMPLETELY SAFE, DIMLY LIT, UNDER-GROUND, MAD SCIENTIST LAB WITH STRANGE GLOWING AND BUBBLING EQUIPMENT.
EWW. THERE'S A WEIRD SLIME ON THE FLOOR. DON'T GO NEAR IT, CHARLIE.
PISH POSH, CAROL. IT'S OKAY.
I'M SURE IT'S JUST SYRUP THAT THE GOOD SCIENTIST SPILLED WHILE HAVING FLAPJACKS FOR BREAKFAST. NOW, LET'S FIND SOME FOOD, I'M STARVING.
I BET THER SOMETHING IN THIS CONT LABELE MATERIAL
SPLORP
CHARLIE, SHE'S RIGHT. THE SLIME LOOKS WRONG.
OH NO! CHARLIE, WHAT ARE YOU DOING??! GET..GET AWAY FROM IT! LOOK OUT FOR THE TENTACLE!
CHARLIEEEEEEEE!
UUUURK!! I DON'T THINK THIS IS BREAKFAST!!
CAROL, SAVE YOURSELF FROM THE MUTANT PANCAKE TENTACLE!!!!
AAAAUUG
ZZZZZ...
BILLY?

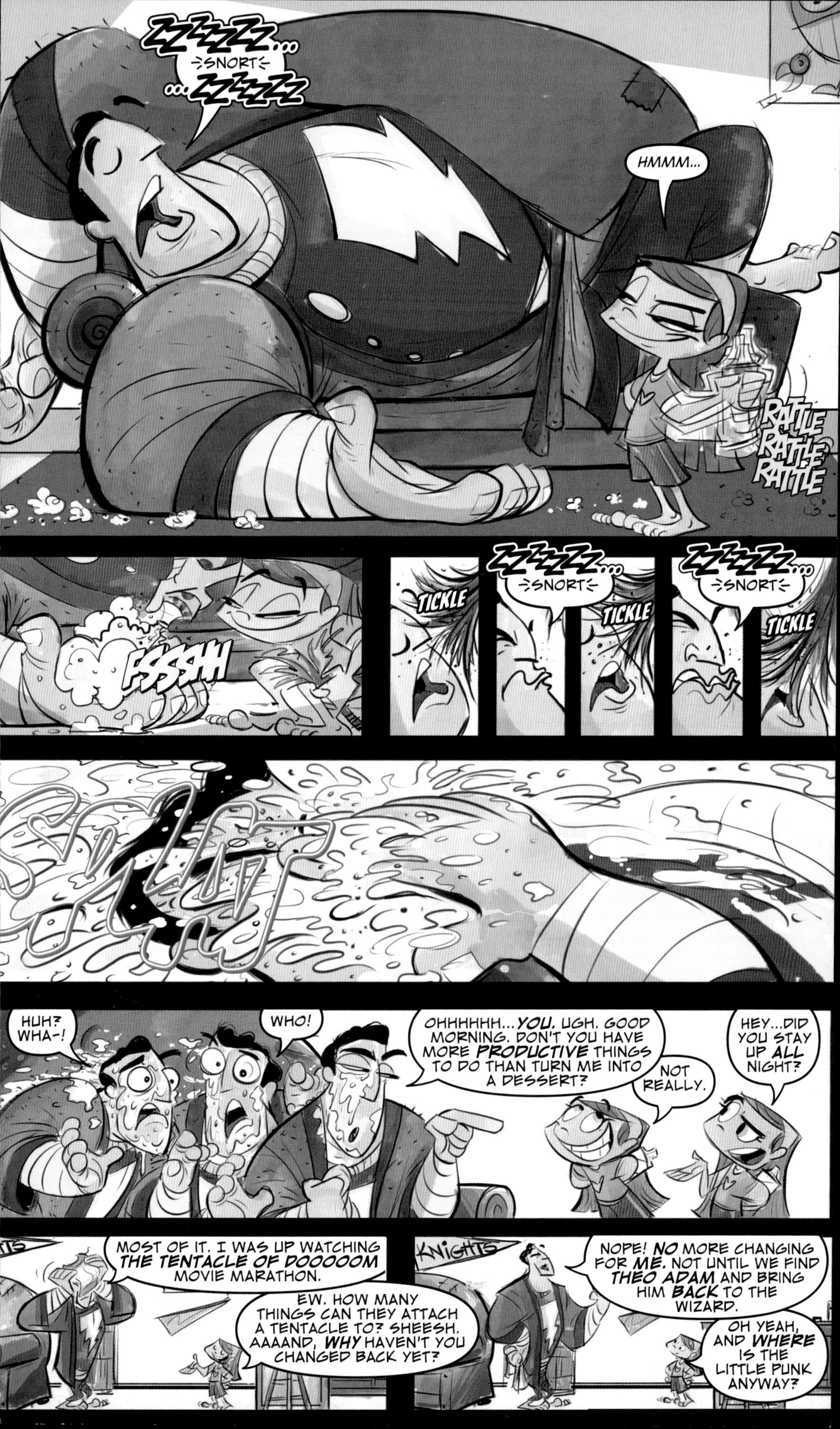
ZZZZZZ...
SNORT
...ZZZZZZ
HMMM...
RATTLE RATTLE RATTLE
FSSSHH
TICKLE
ZZZZZZ...
SNORT
TICKLE
ZZZZZZ...
SNORT
TICKLE
HUH? WHA-!
WHO!
OHHHHHH...YOU. UGH. GOOD MORNING. DON'T YOU HAVE MORE PRODUCTIVE THINGS TO DO THAN TURN ME INTO A DESSERT?
NOT REALLY.
HEY...DID YOU STAY UP ALL NIGHT?
MOST OF IT. I WAS UP WATCHING THE TENTACLE OF DOOOOOM MOVIE MARATHON.
EW. HOW MANY THINGS CAN THEY ATTACH A TENTACLE TO? SHEESH. AAAAND, WHY HAVEN'T YOU CHANGED BACK YET?
NOPE! NO MORE CHANGING FOR ME. NOT UNTIL WE FIND THEO ADAM AND BRING HIM BACK TO THE WIZARD.
OH YEAH, AND WHERE IS THE LITTLE PUNK ANYWAY?

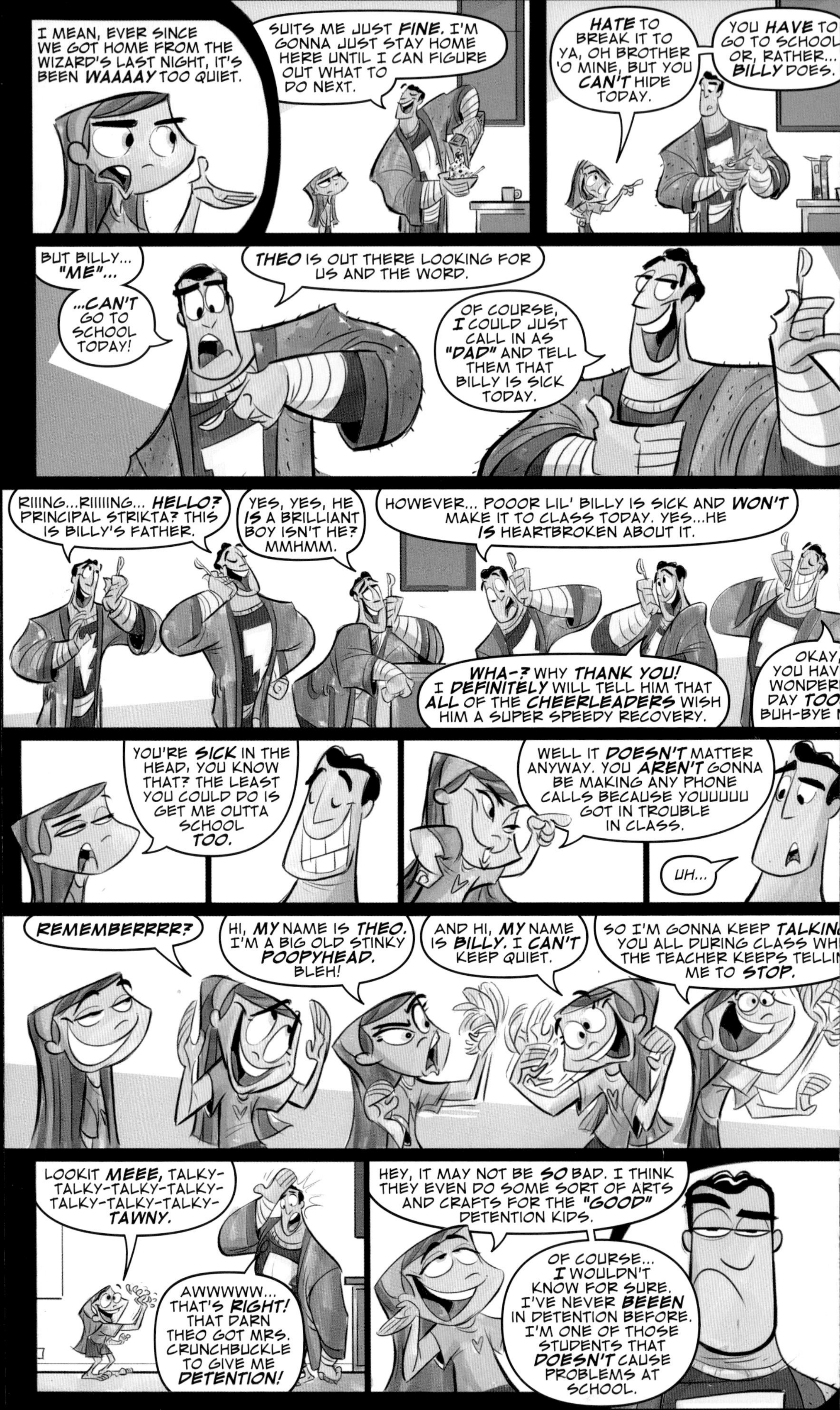

I MEAN, EVER SINCE WE GOT HOME FROM THE WIZARD'S LAST NIGHT, IT'S BEEN WAAAAY TOO QUIET.
SUITS ME JUST FINE. I'M GONNA JUST STAY HOME HERE UNTIL I CAN FIGURE OUT WHAT TO DO NEXT.
HATE TO BREAK IT TO YA, OH BROTHER 'O MINE, BUT YOU CAN'T HIDE TODAY.
YOU HAVE TO GO TO SCHOOL OR, RATHER... BILLY DOES.
BUT BILLY... "ME"...
...CAN'T GO TO SCHOOL TODAY!
THEO IS OUT THERE LOOKING FOR US AND THE WORD.
OF COURSE, I COULD JUST CALL IN AS "DAD" AND TELL THEM THAT BILLY IS SICK TODAY.
RIIING...RIIIING... HELLO? PRINCIPAL STRIKTA? THIS IS BILLY'S FATHER.
YES, YES, HE IS A BRILLIANT BOY ISN'T HE? MMHMM.
HOWEVER... POOOR LIL' BILLY IS SICK AND WON'T MAKE IT TO CLASS TODAY. YES...HE IS HEARTBROKEN ABOUT IT.
WHA-? WHY THANK YOU! I DEFINITELY WILL TELL HIM THAT ALL OF THE CHEERLEADERS WISH HIM A SUPER SPEEDY RECOVERY.
OKAY, YOU HAV WONDER DAY TOO BUH-BYE
YOU'RE SICK IN THE HEAD, YOU KNOW THAT? THE LEAST YOU COULD DO IS GET ME OUTTA SCHOOL TOO.
WELL IT DOESN'T MATTER ANYWAY. YOU AREN'T GONNA BE MAKING ANY PHONE CALLS BECAUSE YOUUUUU GOT IN TROUBLE IN CLASS.
UH...
REMEMBERRRR?
HI, MY NAME IS THEO. I'M A BIG OLD STINKY POOPYHEAD. BLEH!
AND HI, MY NAME IS BILLY. I CAN'T KEEP QUIET.
SO I'M GONNA KEEP TALKIN YOU ALL DURING CLASS WH THE TEACHER KEEPS TELLI ME TO STOP.
LOOKIT MEEE, TALKY-TALKY-TALKY-TALKY-TALKY-TALKY-TALKY-TAWNY.
AWWWWW... THAT'S RIGHT! THAT DARN THEO GOT MRS. CRUNCHBUCKLE TO GIVE ME DETENTION!
HEY, IT MAY NOT BE SO BAD. I THINK THEY EVEN DO SOME SORT OF ARTS AND CRAFTS FOR THE "GOOD" DETENTION KIDS.
OF COURSE... I WOULDN'T KNOW FOR SURE. I'VE NEVER BEEN IN DETENTION BEFORE. I'M ONE OF THOSE STUDENTS THAT DOESN'T CAUSE PROBLEMS AT SCHOOL.

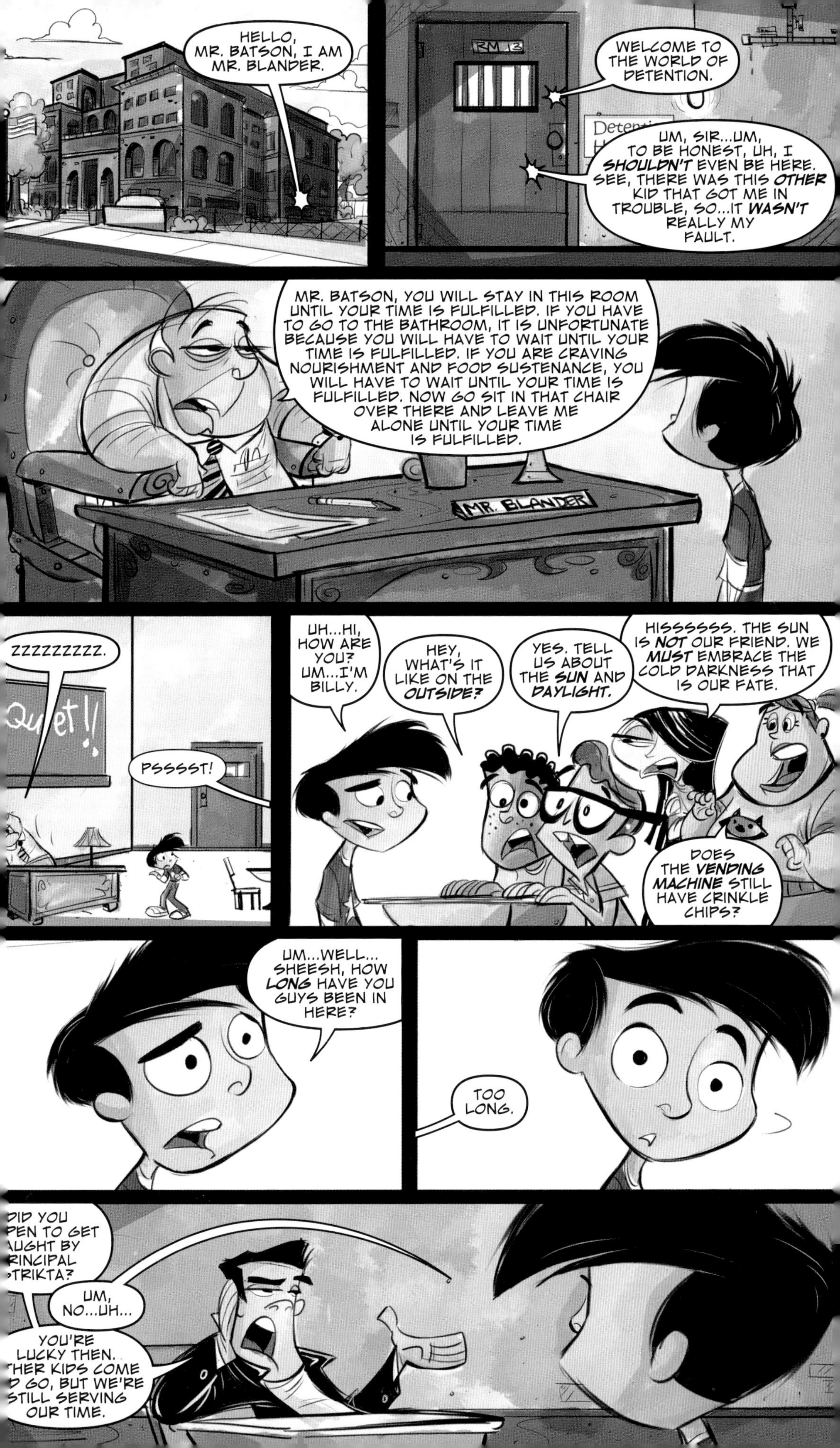
HELLO, MR. BATSON, I AM MR. BLANDER.
RM 13
WELCOME TO THE WORLD OF DETENTION.
UM, SIR...UM, TO BE HONEST, UH, I SHOULDN'T EVEN BE HERE. SEE, THERE WAS THIS OTHER KID THAT GOT ME IN TROUBLE, SO...IT WASN'T REALLY MY FAULT.
MR. BATSON, YOU WILL STAY IN THIS ROOM UNTIL YOUR TIME IS FULFILLED. IF YOU HAVE TO GO TO THE BATHROOM, IT IS UNFORTUNATE BECAUSE YOU WILL HAVE TO WAIT UNTIL YOUR TIME IS FULFILLED. IF YOU ARE CRAVING NOURISHMENT AND FOOD SUSTENANCE, YOU WILL HAVE TO WAIT UNTIL YOUR TIME IS FULFILLED. NOW GO SIT IN THAT CHAIR OVER THERE AND LEAVE ME ALONE UNTIL YOUR TIME IS FULFILLED.
MR. BLANDER
ZZZZZZZZZ.
Quiet!!
PSSSST!
UH...HI, HOW ARE YOU? UM...I'M BILLY.
HEY, WHAT'S IT LIKE ON THE OUTSIDE?
YES. TELL US ABOUT THE SUN AND DAYLIGHT.
HISSSSSS. THE SUN IS NOT OUR FRIEND. WE MUST EMBRACE THE COLD DARKNESS THAT IS OUR FATE.
DOES THE VENDING MACHINE STILL HAVE CRINKLE CHIPS?
UM...WELL... SHEESH, HOW LONG HAVE YOU GUYS BEEN IN HERE?
TOO LONG.
DID YOU PEN TO GET AUGHT BY RINCIPAL STRIKTA?
UM, NO...UH...
YOU'RE LUCKY THEN. THER KIDS COME D GO, BUT WE'RE STILL SERVING OUR TIME.

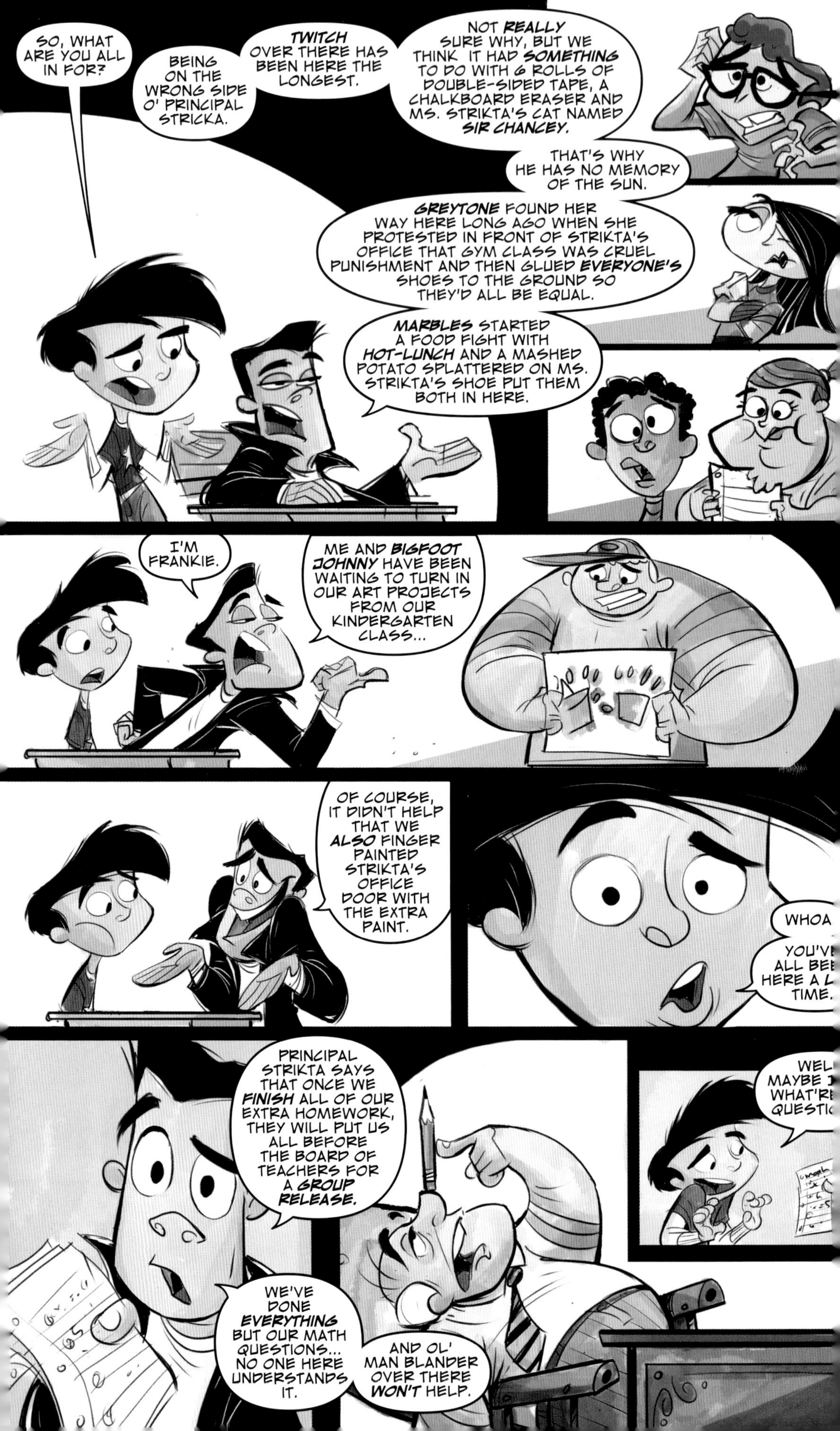
SO, WHAT ARE YOU ALL IN FOR?
BEING ON THE WRONG SIDE O' PRINCIPAL STRICKA.
TWITCH OVER THERE HAS BEEN HERE THE LONGEST.
NOT REALLY SURE WHY, BUT WE THINK IT HAD SOMETHING TO DO WITH 6 ROLLS OF DOUBLE-SIDED TAPE, A CHALKBOARD ERASER AND MS. STRIKTA'S CAT NAMED SIR CHANCEY.
THAT'S WHY HE HAS NO MEMORY OF THE SUN.
GREYTONE FOUND HER WAY HERE LONG AGO WHEN SHE PROTESTED IN FRONT OF STRIKTA'S OFFICE THAT GYM CLASS WAS CRUEL PUNISHMENT AND THEN GLUED EVERYONE'S SHOES TO THE GROUND SO THEY'D ALL BE EQUAL.
MARBLES STARTED A FOOD FIGHT WITH HOT-LUNCH AND A MASHED POTATO SPLATTERED ON MS. STRIKTA'S SHOE PUT THEM BOTH IN HERE.
I'M FRANKIE.
ME AND BIGFOOT JOHNNY HAVE BEEN WAITING TO TURN IN OUR ART PROJECTS FROM OUR KINDERGARTEN CLASS...
OF COURSE, IT DIDN'T HELP THAT WE ALSO FINGER PAINTED STRIKTA'S OFFICE DOOR WITH THE EXTRA PAINT.
WHOA
YOU'VE ALL BEE HERE A L TIME.
PRINCIPAL STRIKTA SAYS THAT ONCE WE FINISH ALL OF OUR EXTRA HOMEWORK, THEY WILL PUT US ALL BEFORE THE BOARD OF TEACHERS FOR A GROUP RELEASE.
WE'VE DONE EVERYTHING BUT OUR MATH QUESTIONS... NO ONE HERE UNDERSTANDS IT.
AND OL' MAN BLANDER OVER THERE WON'T HELP.
WEL MAYBE I WHAT'RE QUESTIC

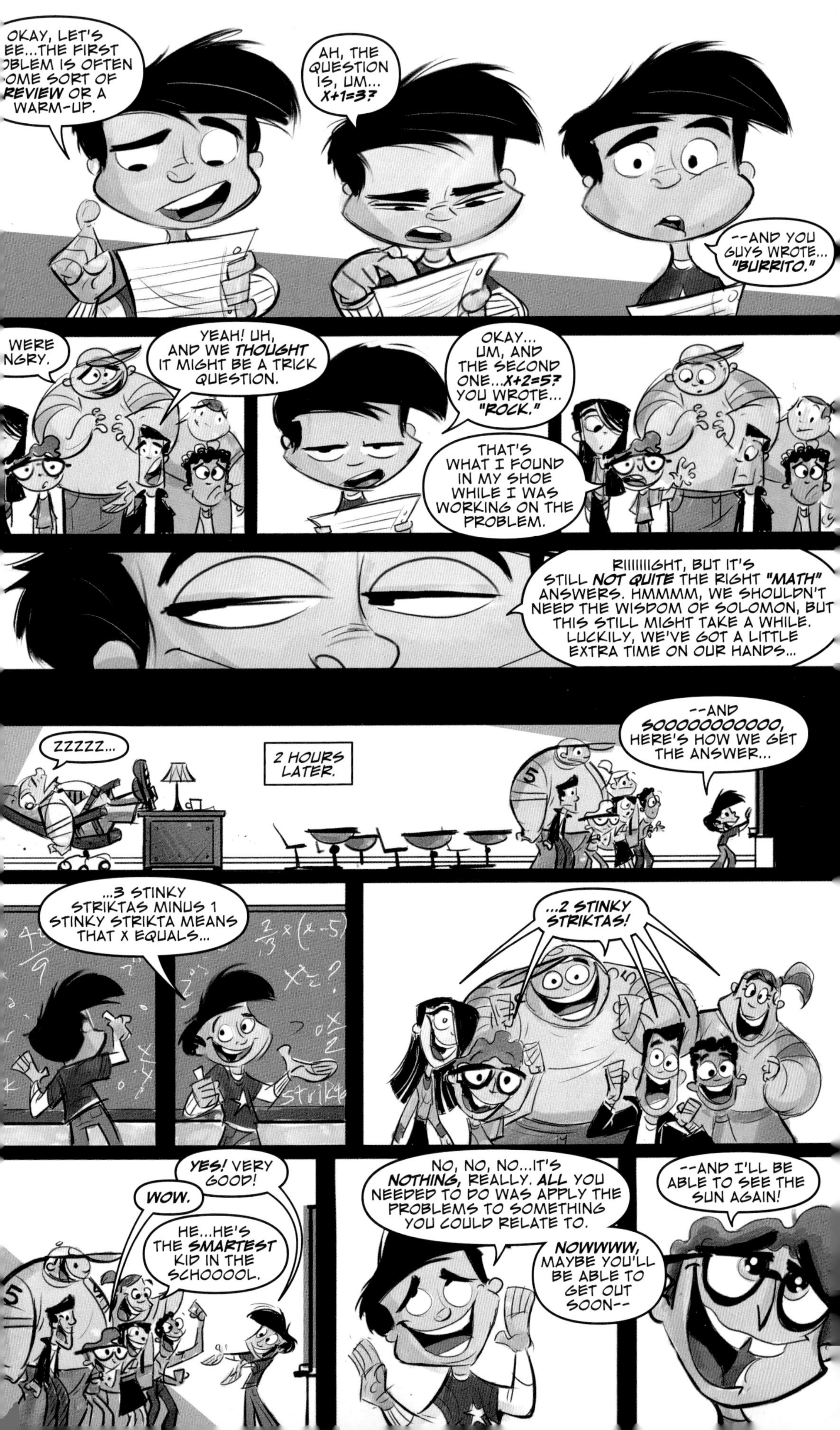

OKAY, LET'S
EE...THE FIRST
OBLEM IS OFTEN
OME SORT OF
REVIEW OR A
WARM-UP.
AH, THE QUESTION IS, UM... X+1=3?
--AND YOU GUYS WROTE... "BURRITO."
WERE
NGRY.
YEAH! UH, AND WE THOUGHT IT MIGHT BE A TRICK QUESTION.
OKAY... UM, AND THE SECOND ONE...X+2=5? YOU WROTE... "ROCK."
THAT'S WHAT I FOUND IN MY SHOE WHILE I WAS WORKING ON THE PROBLEM.
RIIIIIIIGHT, BUT IT'S STILL NOT QUITE THE RIGHT "MATH" ANSWERS. HMMMM, WE SHOULDN'T NEED THE WISDOM OF SOLOMON, BUT THIS STILL MIGHT TAKE A WHILE. LUCKILY, WE'VE GOT A LITTLE EXTRA TIME ON OUR HANDS...
ZZZZZ...
2 HOURS LATER.
--AND SOOOOOOOOOOO, HERE'S HOW WE GET THE ANSWER...
...3 STINKY STRIKTAS MINUS 1 STINKY STRIKTA MEANS THAT X EQUALS...
...2 STINKY STRIKTAS!
YES! VERY GOOD!
WOW.
HE...HE'S THE SMARTEST KID IN THE SCHOOOOL.
NO, NO, NO...IT'S NOTHING, REALLY. ALL YOU NEEDED TO DO WAS APPLY THE PROBLEMS TO SOMETHING YOU COULD RELATE TO.
NOWWWW, MAYBE YOU'LL BE ABLE TO GET OUT SOON--
--AND I'LL BE ABLE TO SEE THE SUN AGAIN!

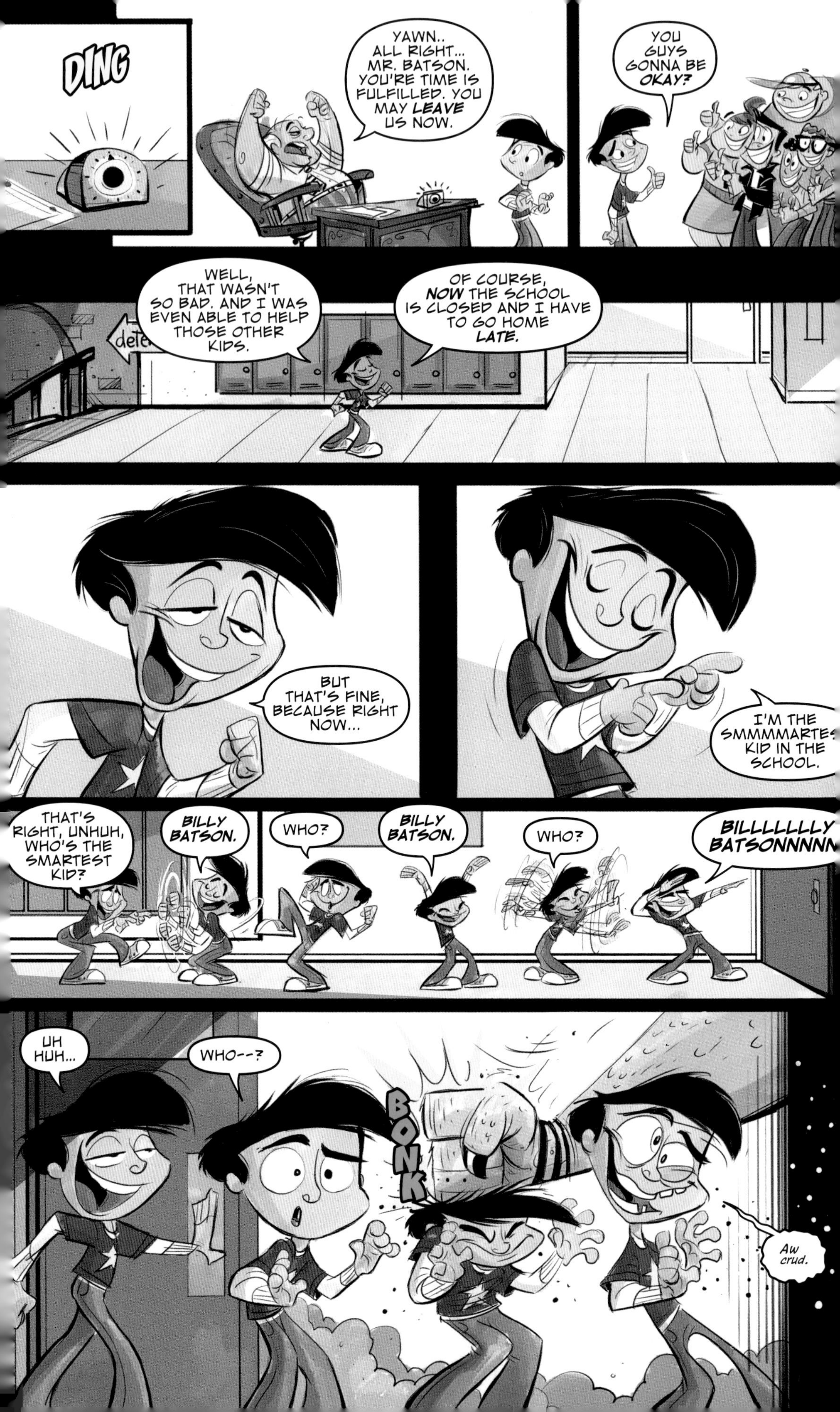
DING
YAWN.. ALL RIGHT... MR. BATSON. YOU'RE TIME IS FULFILLED. YOU MAY LEAVE US NOW.
YOU GUYS GONNA BE OKAY?
WELL, THAT WASN'T SO BAD. AND I WAS EVEN ABLE TO HELP THOSE OTHER KIDS.
OF COURSE, NOW THE SCHOOL IS CLOSED AND I HAVE TO GO HOME LATE.
BUT THAT'S FINE, BECAUSE RIGHT NOW...
I'M THE SMMMMARTES KID IN THE SCHOOL.
THAT'S RIGHT, UNHUH, WHO'S THE SMARTEST KID?
BILLY BATSON.
WHO?
BILLY BATSON.
WHO?
BILLLLLLLY BATSONNNNN
UH HUH...
WHO--?
BONK
Aw crud.

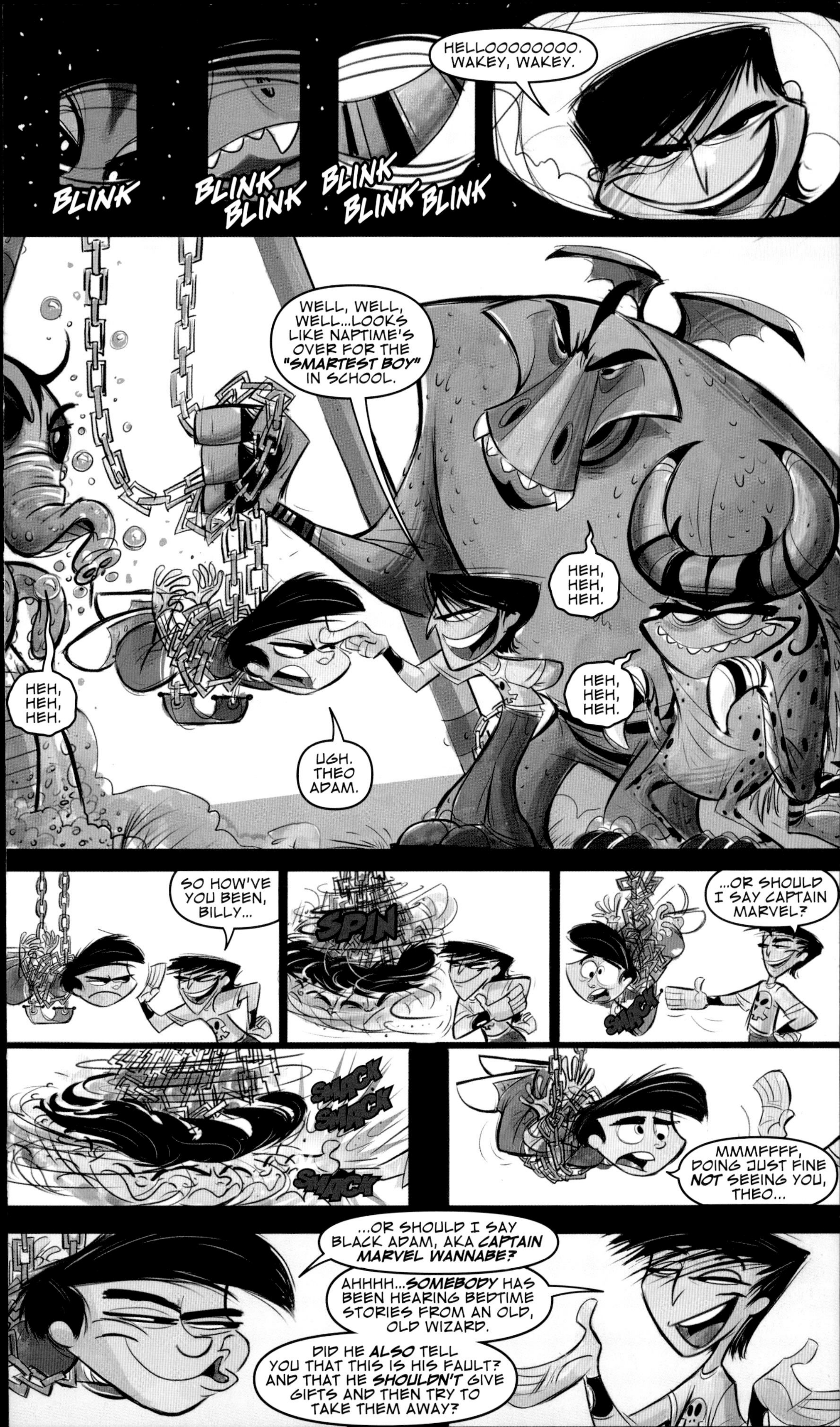
BLINK
BLINK BLINK
BLINK BLINK BLINK
HELLOOOOOOOO. WAKEY, WAKEY.
WELL, WELL, WELL...LOOKS LIKE NAPTIME'S OVER FOR THE "SMARTEST BOY" IN SCHOOL.
HEH, HEH, HEH.
HEH, HEH, HEH.
HEH, HEH, HEH.
UGH. THEO ADAM.
SO HOW'VE YOU BEEN, BILLY...
SPIN
...OR SHOULD I SAY CAPTAIN MARVEL?
SMACK
SMACK
SMACK
SMACK
MMMFFFF, DOING JUST FINE NOT SEEING YOU, THEO...
...OR SHOULD I SAY BLACK ADAM, AKA CAPTAIN MARVEL WANNABE?
AHHHH...SOMEBODY HAS BEEN HEARING BEDTIME STORIES FROM AN OLD, OLD WIZARD.
DID HE ALSO TELL YOU THAT THIS IS HIS FAULT? AND THAT HE SHOULDN'T GIVE GIFTS AND THEN TRY TO TAKE THEM AWAY?

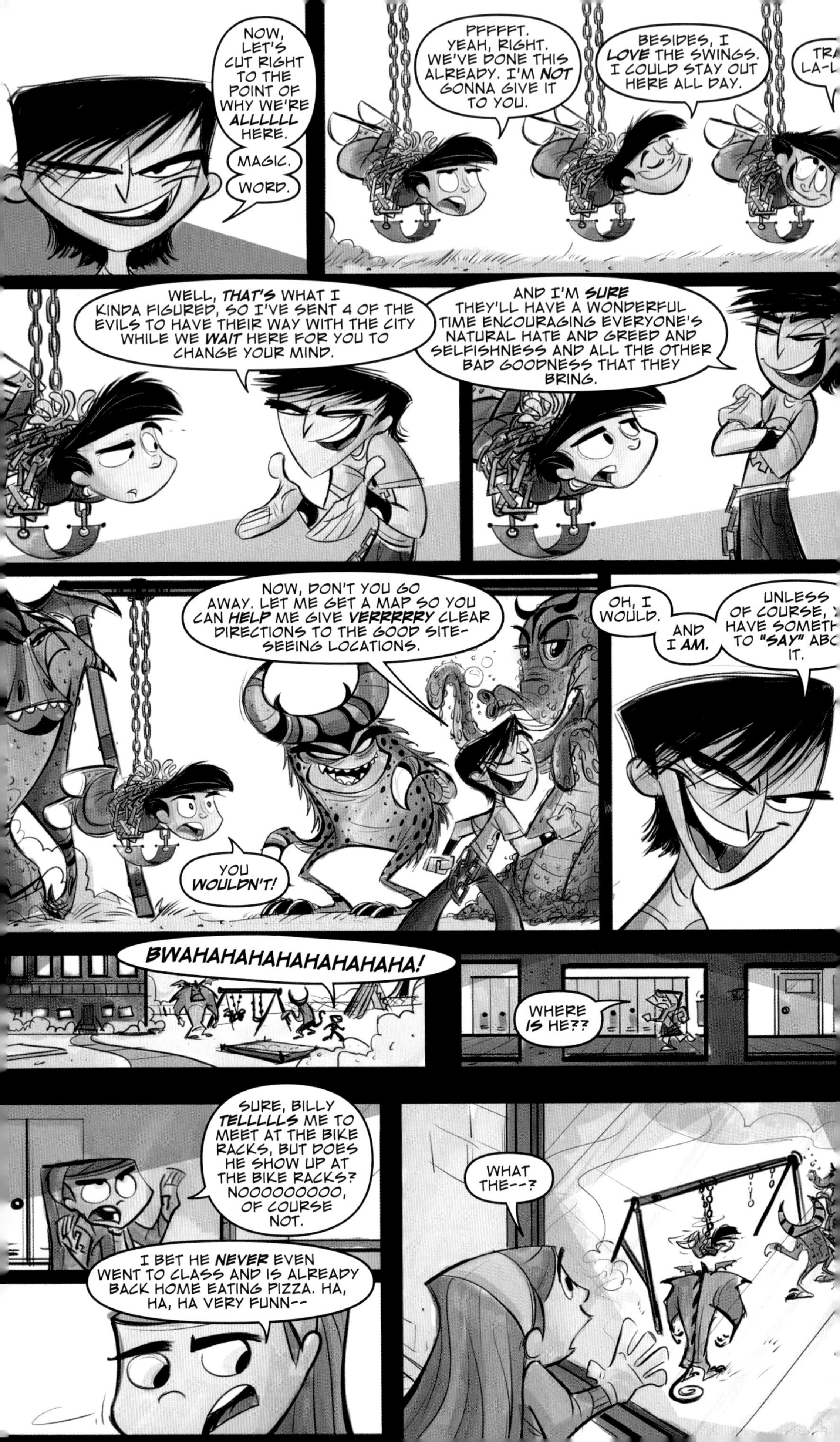

NOW, LET'S CUT RIGHT TO THE POINT OF WHY WE'RE ALLLLLL HERE.
MAGIC.
WORD.
PFFFFT. YEAH, RIGHT. WE'VE DONE THIS ALREADY. I'M NOT GONNA GIVE IT TO YOU.
BESIDES, I LOVE THE SWINGS. I COULD STAY OUT HERE ALL DAY.
TRA LA-L
WELL, THAT'S WHAT I KINDA FIGURED, SO I'VE SENT 4 OF THE EVILS TO HAVE THEIR WAY WITH THE CITY WHILE WE WAIT HERE FOR YOU TO CHANGE YOUR MIND.
AND I'M SURE THEY'LL HAVE A WONDERFUL TIME ENCOURAGING EVERYONE'S NATURAL HATE AND GREED AND SELFISHNESS AND ALL THE OTHER BAD GOODNESS THAT THEY BRING.
NOW, DON'T YOU GO AWAY. LET ME GET A MAP SO YOU CAN HELP ME GIVE VERRRRRY CLEAR DIRECTIONS TO THE GOOD SITE-SEEING LOCATIONS.
YOU WOULDN'T!
OH, I WOULD.
AND I AM.
UNLESS OF COURSE, HAVE SOMETH TO "SAY" ABO IT.
BWAHAHAHAHAHAHAHAHA!
WHERE IS HE??
SURE, BILLY TELLLLLS ME TO MEET AT THE BIKE RACKS, BUT DOES HE SHOW UP AT THE BIKE RACKS? NOOOOOOOOO, OF COURSE NOT.
I BET HE NEVER EVEN WENT TO CLASS AND IS ALREADY BACK HOME EATING PIZZA. HA, HA, HA VERY FUNN--
WHAT THE--?

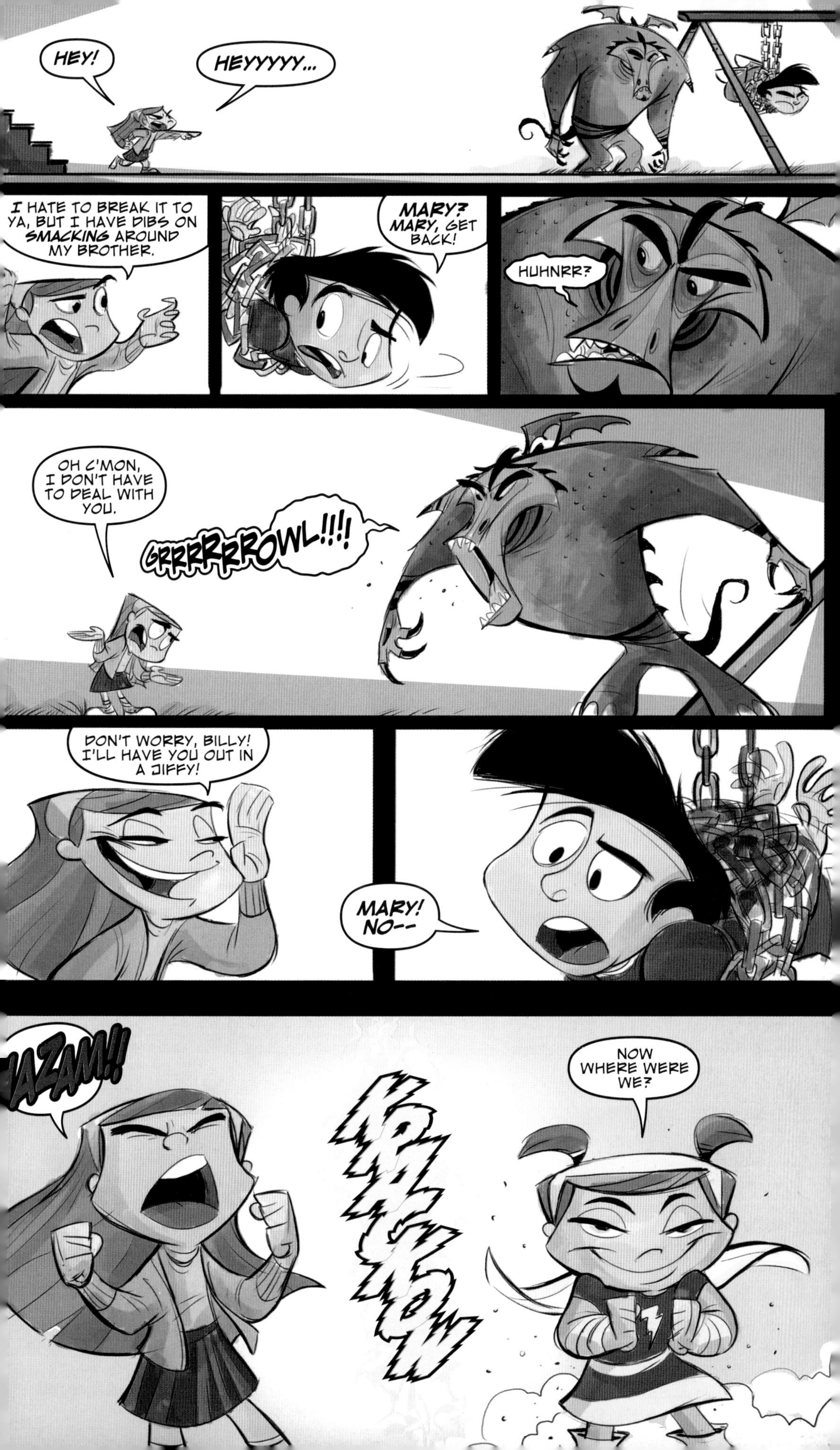
HEY!
HEYYYYY...
I HATE TO BREAK IT TO YA, BUT I HAVE DIBS ON SMACKING AROUND MY BROTHER.
MARY? MARY, GET BACK!
HUHNRR?
OH C'MON, I DON'T HAVE TO DEAL WITH YOU.
GRRRRRROWL!!!!
DON'T WORRY, BILLY! I'LL HAVE YOU OUT IN A JIFFY!
MARY! NO--
AZAM!!
KA-THOOM
NOW WHERE WERE WE?

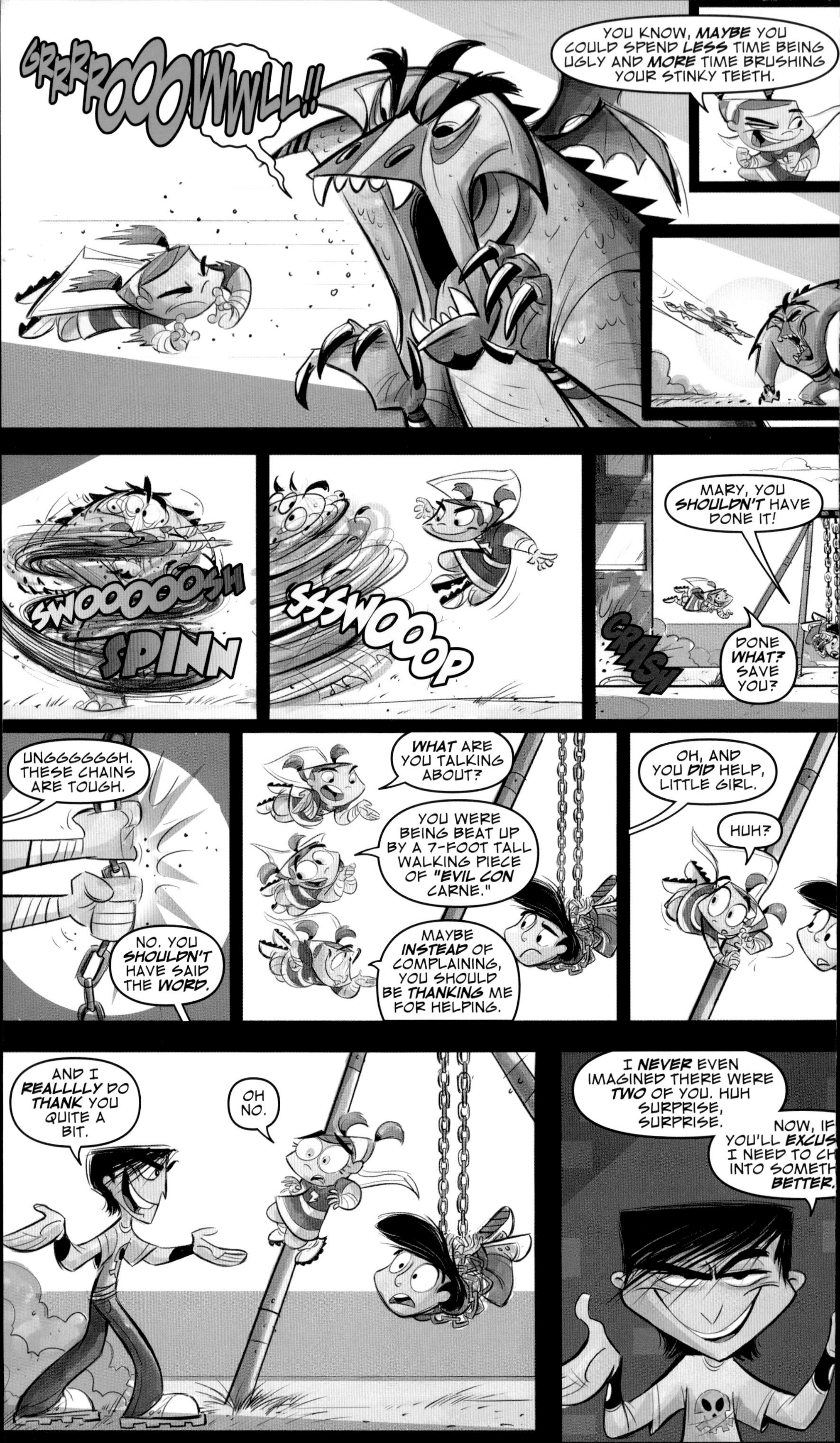
GRRRROOOWWLL!!
YOU KNOW, MAYBE YOU COULD SPEND LESS TIME BEING UGLY AND MORE TIME BRUSHING YOUR STINKY TEETH.
SWOOOOOOSH
SPINN
SSSWOOOOP
MARY, YOU SHOULDN'T HAVE DONE IT!
CRASH
DONE WHAT? SAVE YOU?
UNGGGGGGH. THESE CHAINS ARE TOUGH.
NO. YOU SHOULDN'T HAVE SAID THE WORD.
WHAT ARE YOU TALKING ABOUT?
YOU WERE BEING BEAT UP BY A 7-FOOT TALL WALKING PIECE OF "EVIL CON CARNE."
MAYBE INSTEAD OF COMPLAINING, YOU SHOULD BE THANKING ME FOR HELPING.
OH, AND YOU DID HELP, LITTLE GIRL.
HUH?
AND I REALLLLY DO THANK YOU QUITE A BIT.
OH NO.
I NEVER EVEN IMAGINED THERE WERE TWO OF YOU. HUH SURPRISE, SURPRISE.

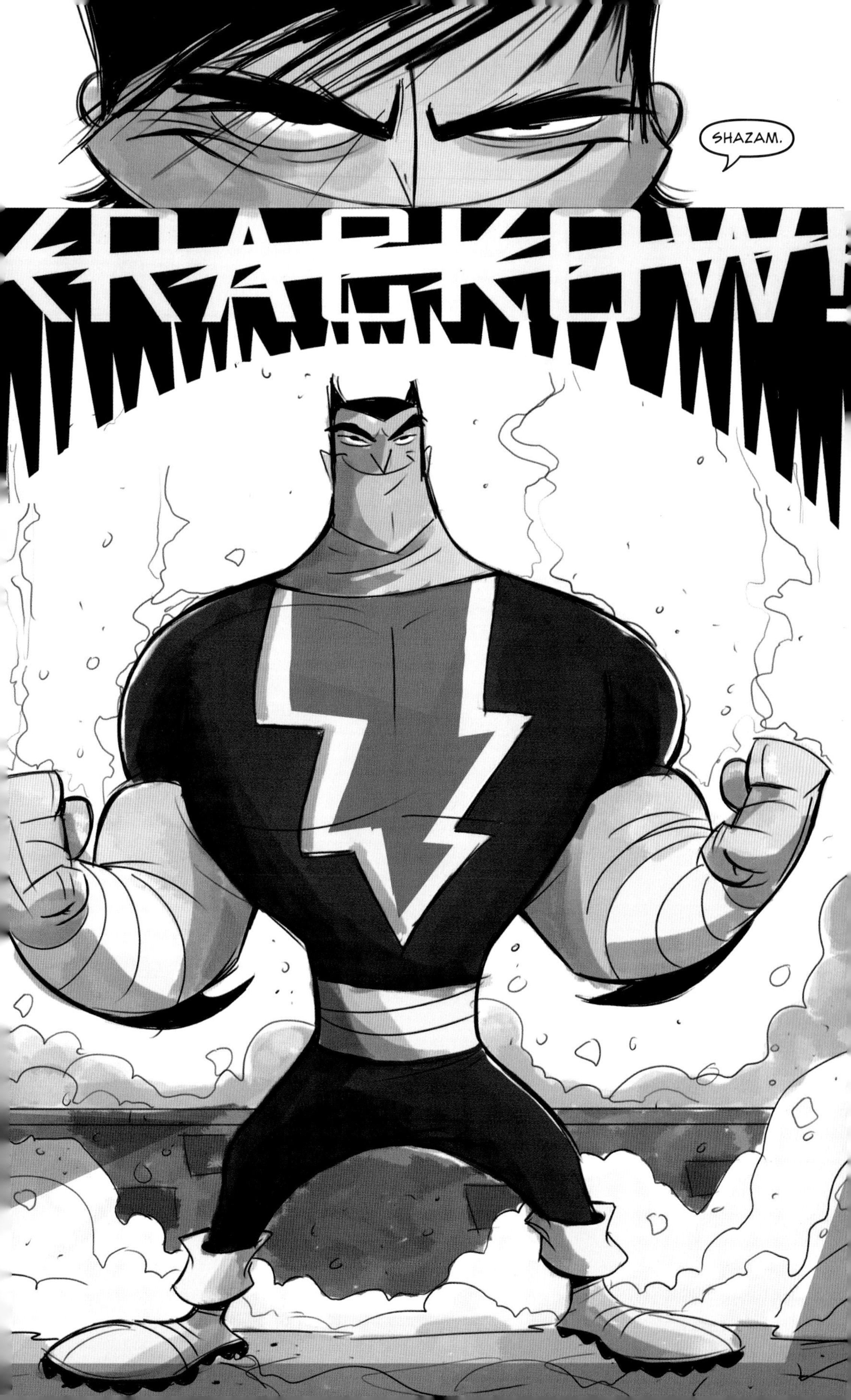
SHAZAM.
KRAKKOW!

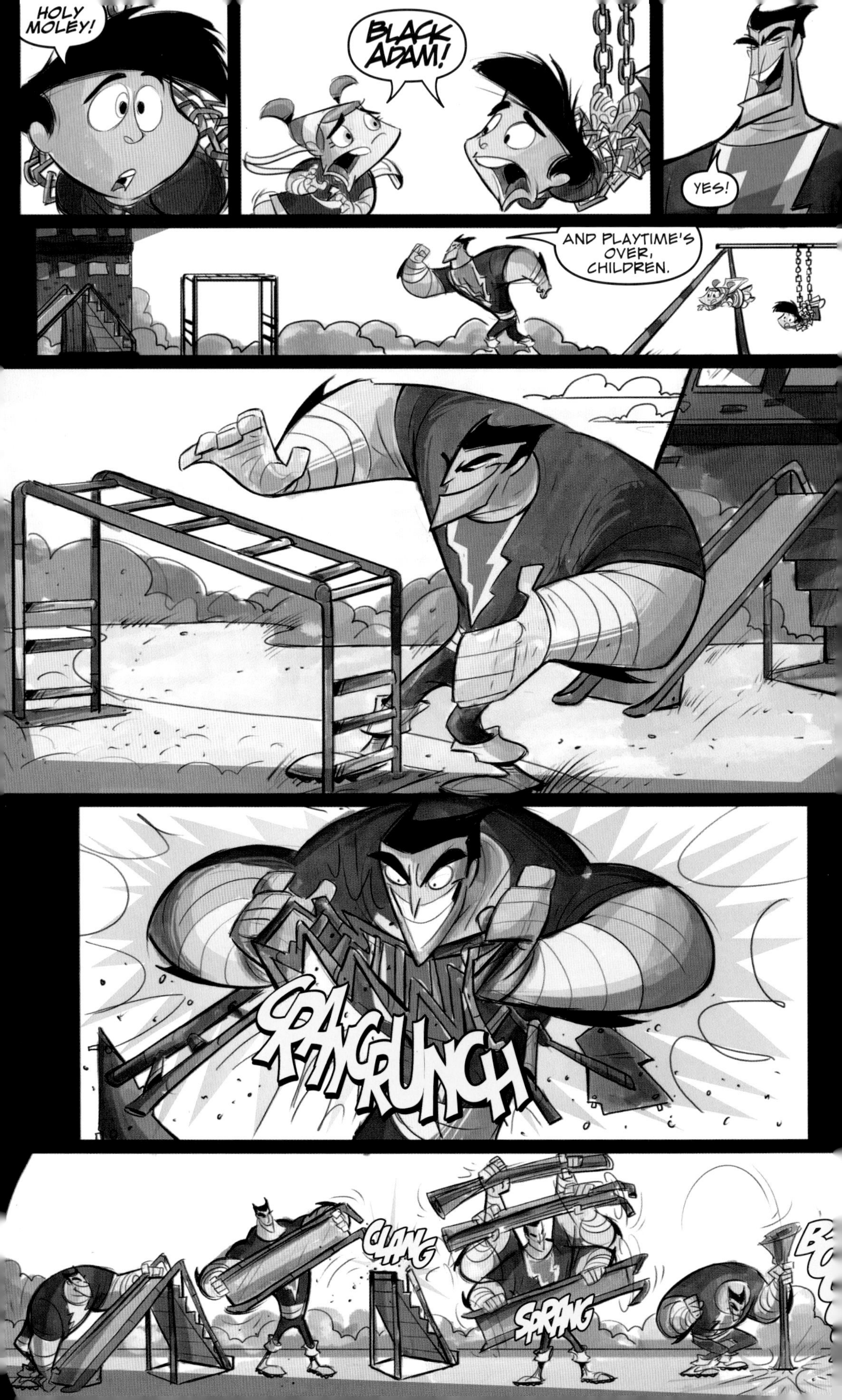
HOLY MOLEY!
BLACK ADAM!
YES!
AND PLAYTIME'S OVER, CHILDREN.
CRANGRUNCH
CLANG
SPRANG

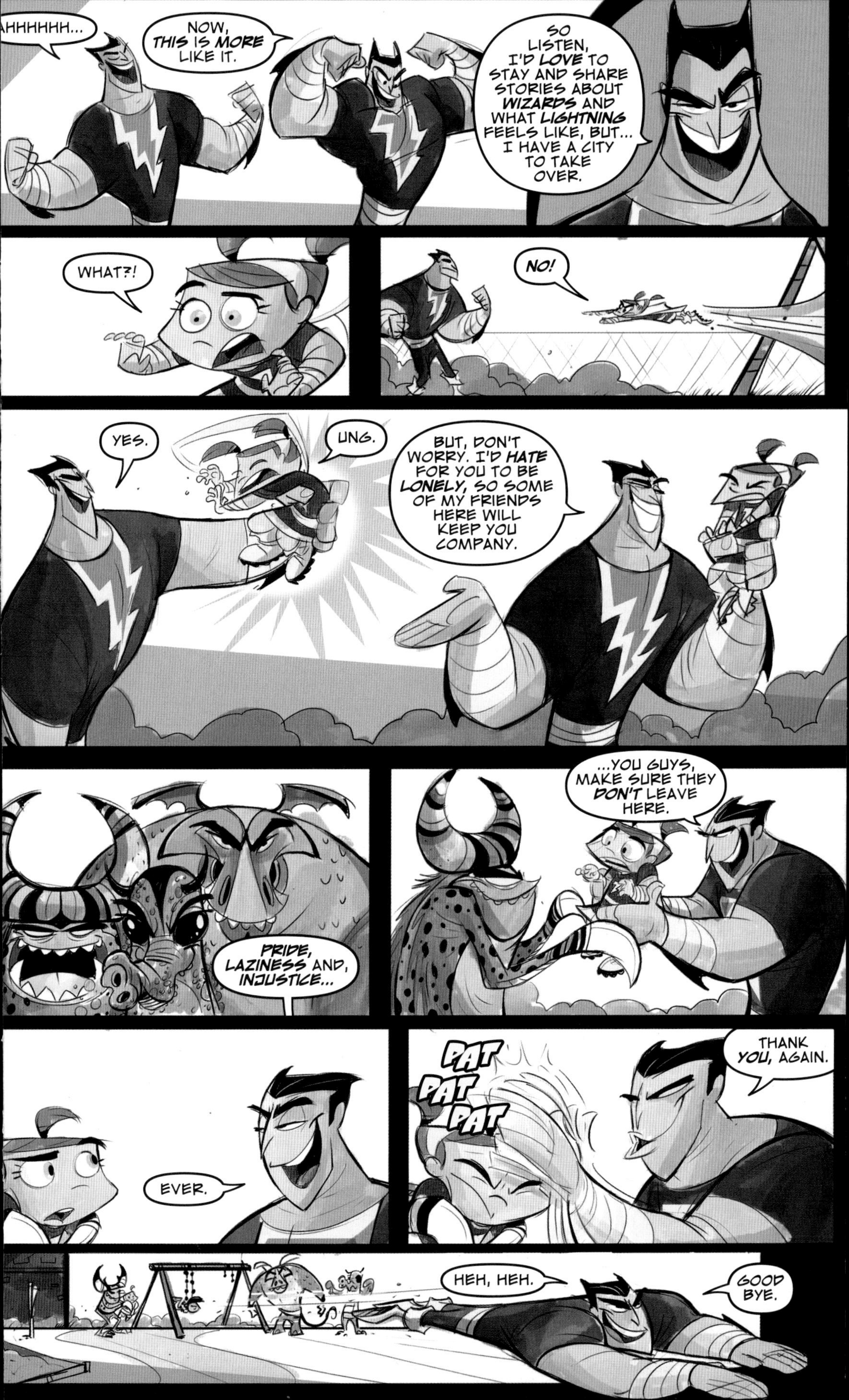
AHHHHHH...
NOW, THIS IS MORE LIKE IT.
SO LISTEN, I'D LOVE TO STAY AND SHARE STORIES ABOUT WIZARDS AND WHAT LIGHTNING FEELS LIKE, BUT... I HAVE A CITY TO TAKE OVER.
WHAT?!
NO!
YES.
UNG.
BUT, DON'T WORRY. I'D HATE FOR YOU TO BE LONELY, SO SOME OF MY FRIENDS HERE WILL KEEP YOU COMPANY.
PRIDE, LAZINESS AND, INJUSTICE...
...YOU GUYS, MAKE SURE THEY DON'T LEAVE HERE.
EVER.
PAT PAT PAT
THANK YOU, AGAIN.
HEH, HEH.
GOOD BYE.

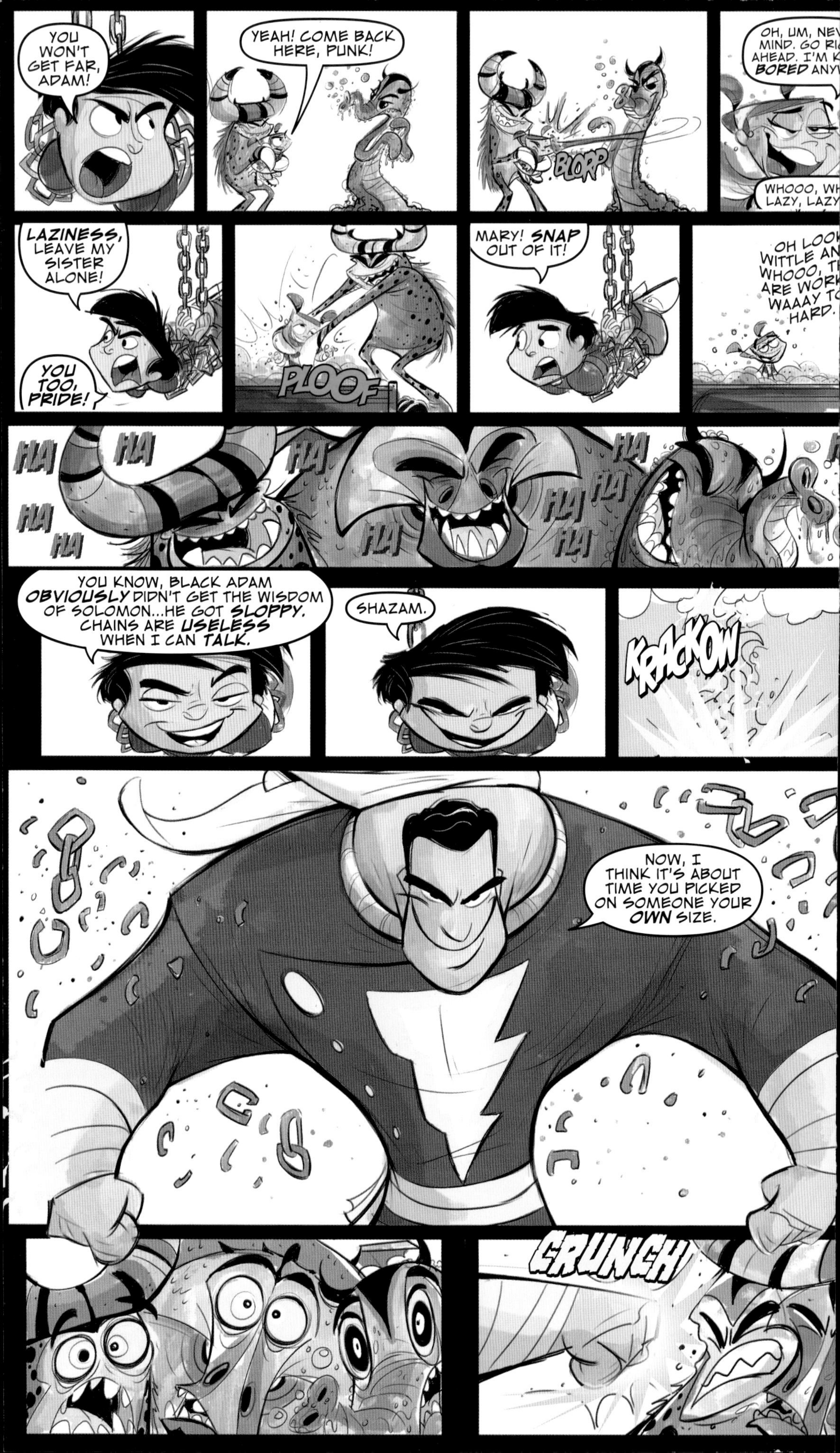
YOU WON'T GET FAR, ADAM!
YEAH! COME BACK HERE, PUNK!
BLORP
OH, UM, NEV MIND. GO RI AHEAD. I'M K BORED ANYW
WHOOO, WH LAZY, LAZY
LAZINESS, LEAVE MY SISTER ALONE!
YOU TOO, PRIDE!
PLOOF
MARY! SNAP OUT OF IT!
OH LOOK WITTLE AN WHOOO, TH ARE WORK WAAAY TO HARD.
HA HA HA HA HA HA HA HA HA HA HA
YOU KNOW, BLACK ADAM OBVIOUSLY DIDN'T GET THE WISDOM OF SOLOMON...HE GOT SLOPPY. CHAINS ARE USELESS WHEN I CAN TALK.
SHAZAM.
KRACKOW
NOW, I THINK IT'S ABOUT TIME YOU PICKED ON SOMEONE YOUR OWN SIZE.
CRUNCH

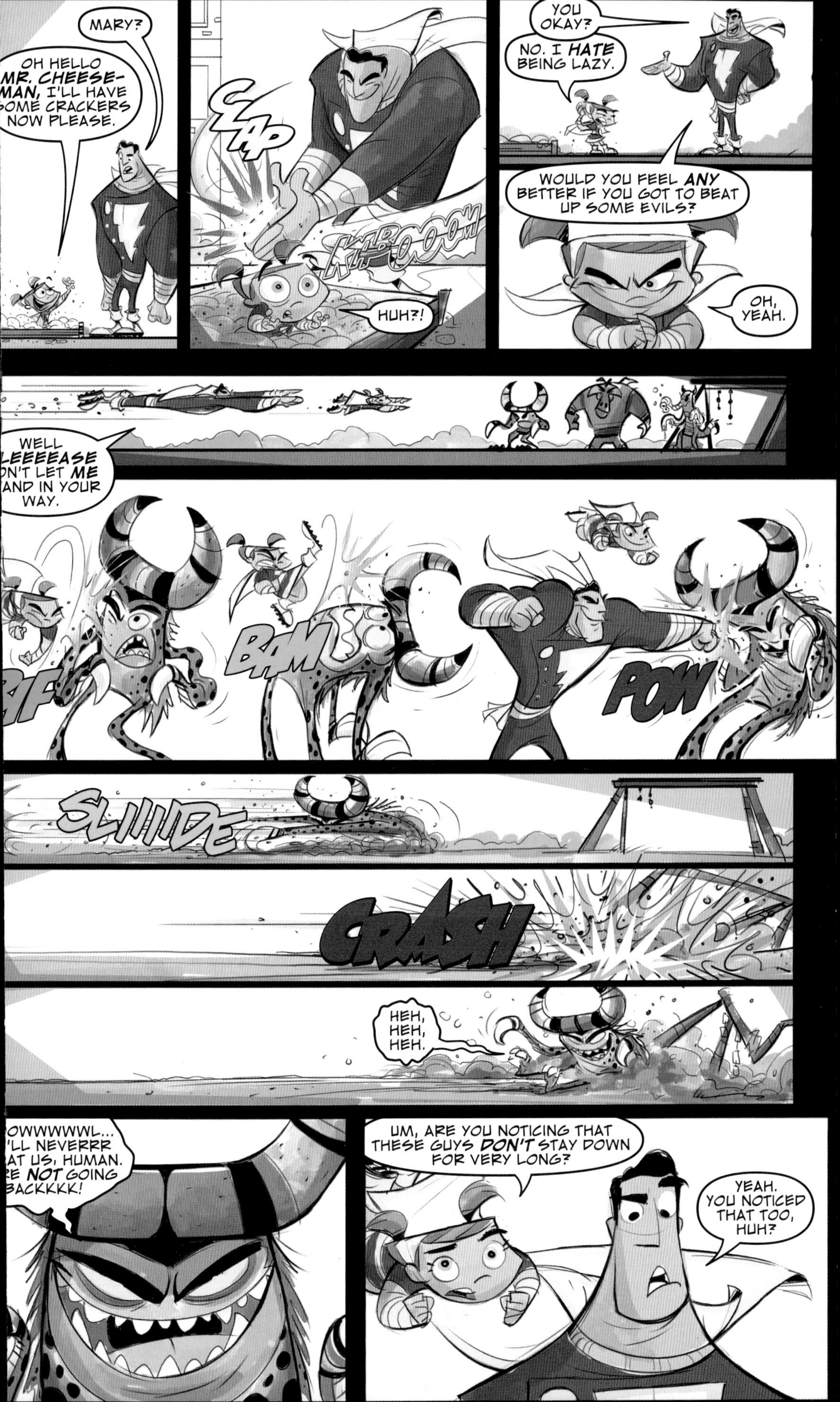
MARY?
OH HELLO MR. CHEESE-MAN, I'LL HAVE SOME CRACKERS NOW PLEASE.
CLAP
KABOOOM
HUH?!
YOU OKAY?
NO. I HATE BEING LAZY.
WOULD YOU FEEL ANY BETTER IF YOU GOT TO BEAT UP SOME EVILS?
OH, YEAH.
WELL LEEEEASE ON'T LET ME AND IN YOUR WAY.
BAM
POW
SLIIIIDE
CRASH
HEH, HEH, HEH.
OWWWWWL... 'LL NEVERRR AT US, HUMAN. E NOT GOING BACKKKK!
UM, ARE YOU NOTICING THAT THESE GUYS DON'T STAY DOWN FOR VERY LONG?
YEAH. YOU NOTICED THAT TOO, HUH?

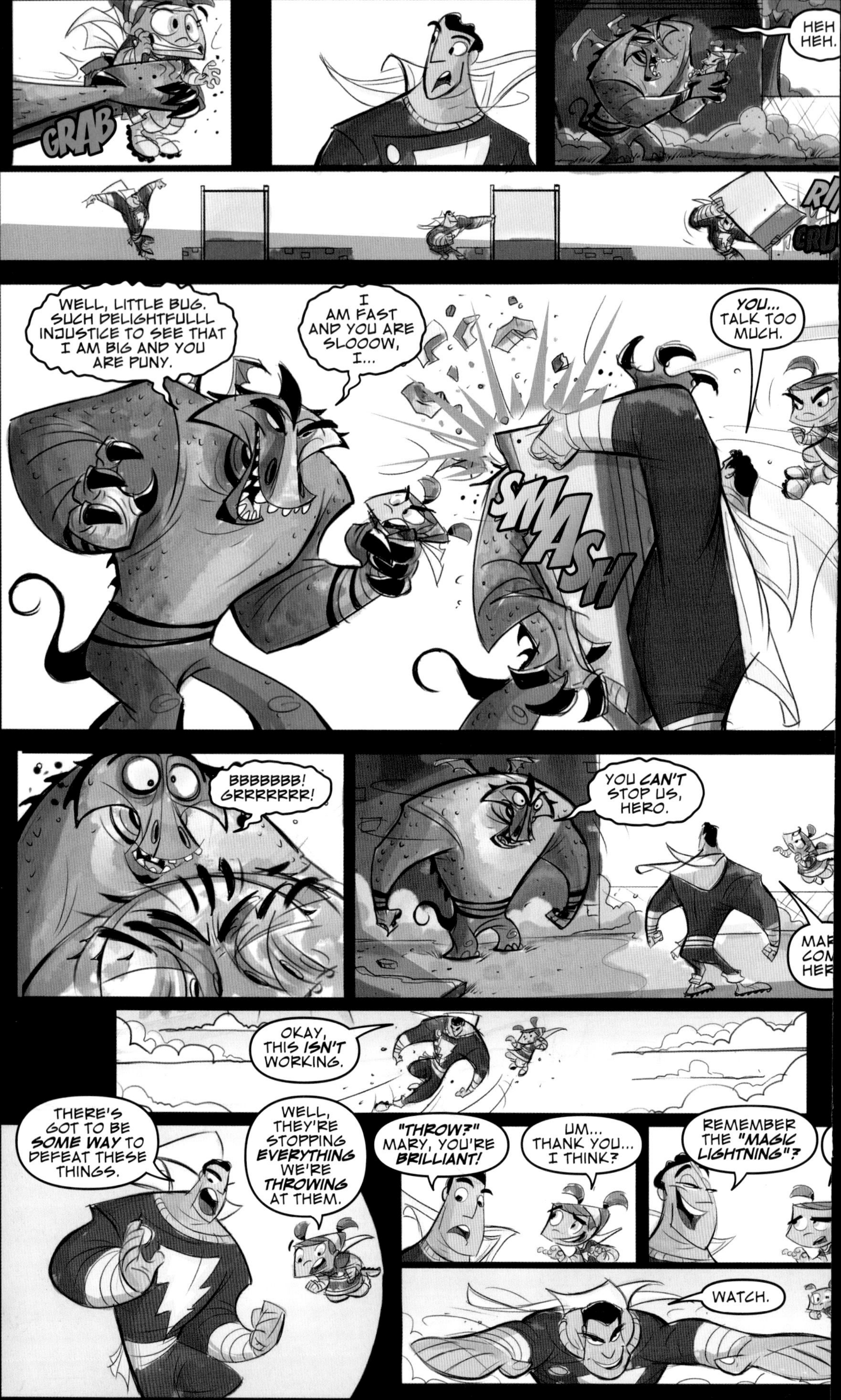

GRAB
HEH HEH.
WELL, LITTLE BUG. SUCH DELIGHTFULLL INJUSTICE TO SEE THAT I AM BIG AND YOU ARE PUNY.
I AM FAST AND YOU ARE SLOOOW, I...
SMASH
YOU... TALK TOO MUCH.
BBBBBBB! GRRRRRRR!
YOU CAN'T STOP US, HERO.
OKAY, THIS ISN'T WORKING.
THERE'S GOT TO BE SOME WAY TO DEFEAT THESE THINGS.
WELL, THEY'RE STOPPING EVERYTHING WE'RE THROWING AT THEM.
"THROW?" MARY, YOU'RE BRILLIANT!
UM... THANK YOU... I THINK?
REMEMBER THE "MAGIC LIGHTNING"?
WATCH.

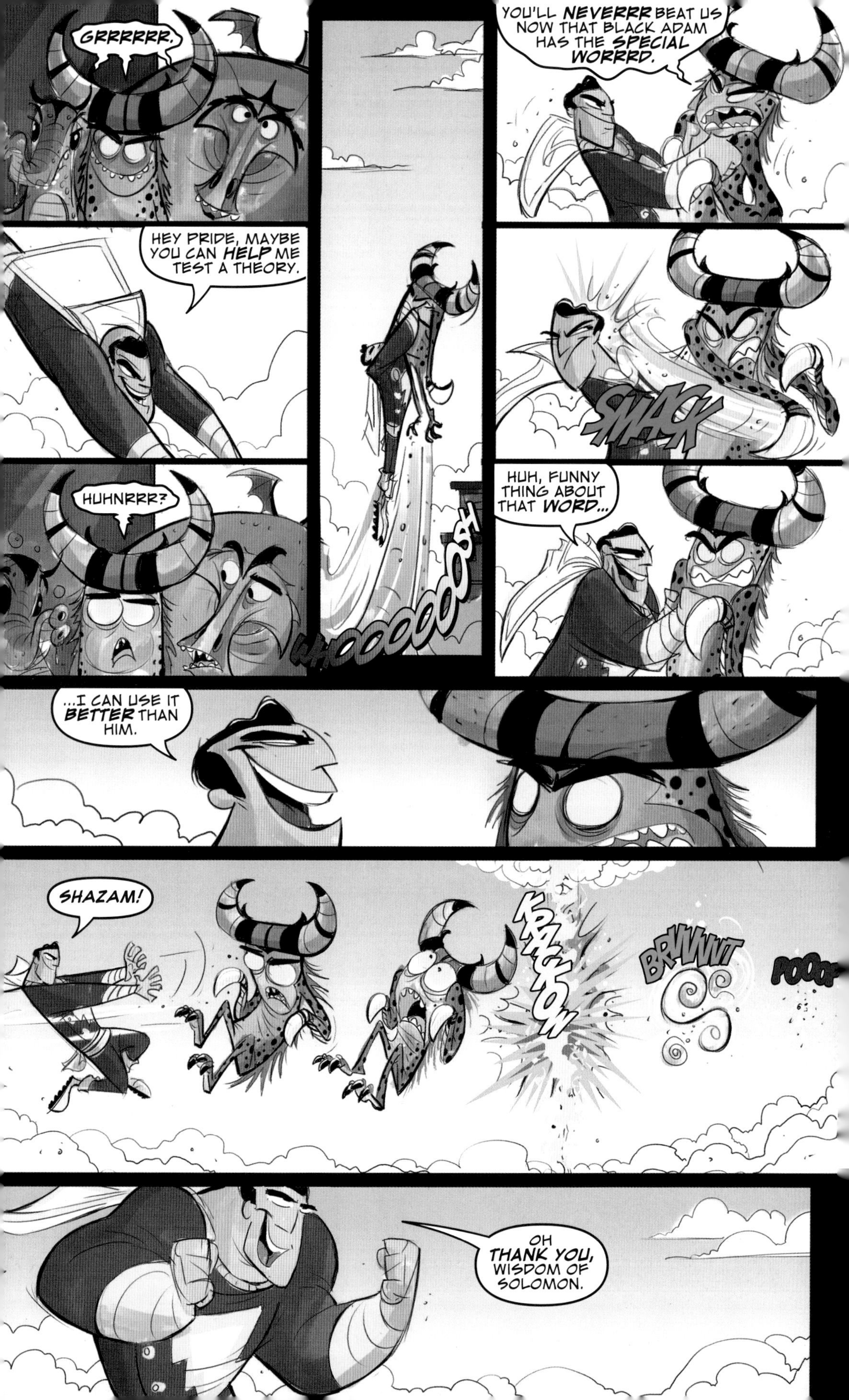
GRRRRRR.
YOU'LL **NEVERRR** BEAT US NOW THAT BLACK ADAM HAS THE **SPECIAL WORRRD.**
HEY PRIDE, MAYBE YOU CAN **HELP** ME TEST A THEORY.
SMACK
HUHNRRR?
WHOOOOOOOOSH
HUH, FUNNY THING ABOUT THAT **WORD**...
...I CAN USE IT **BETTER** THAN HIM.
SHAZAM!
KRA-KOW
BRVVVVT
POOOF
OH **THANK YOU,** WISDOM OF SOLOMON.

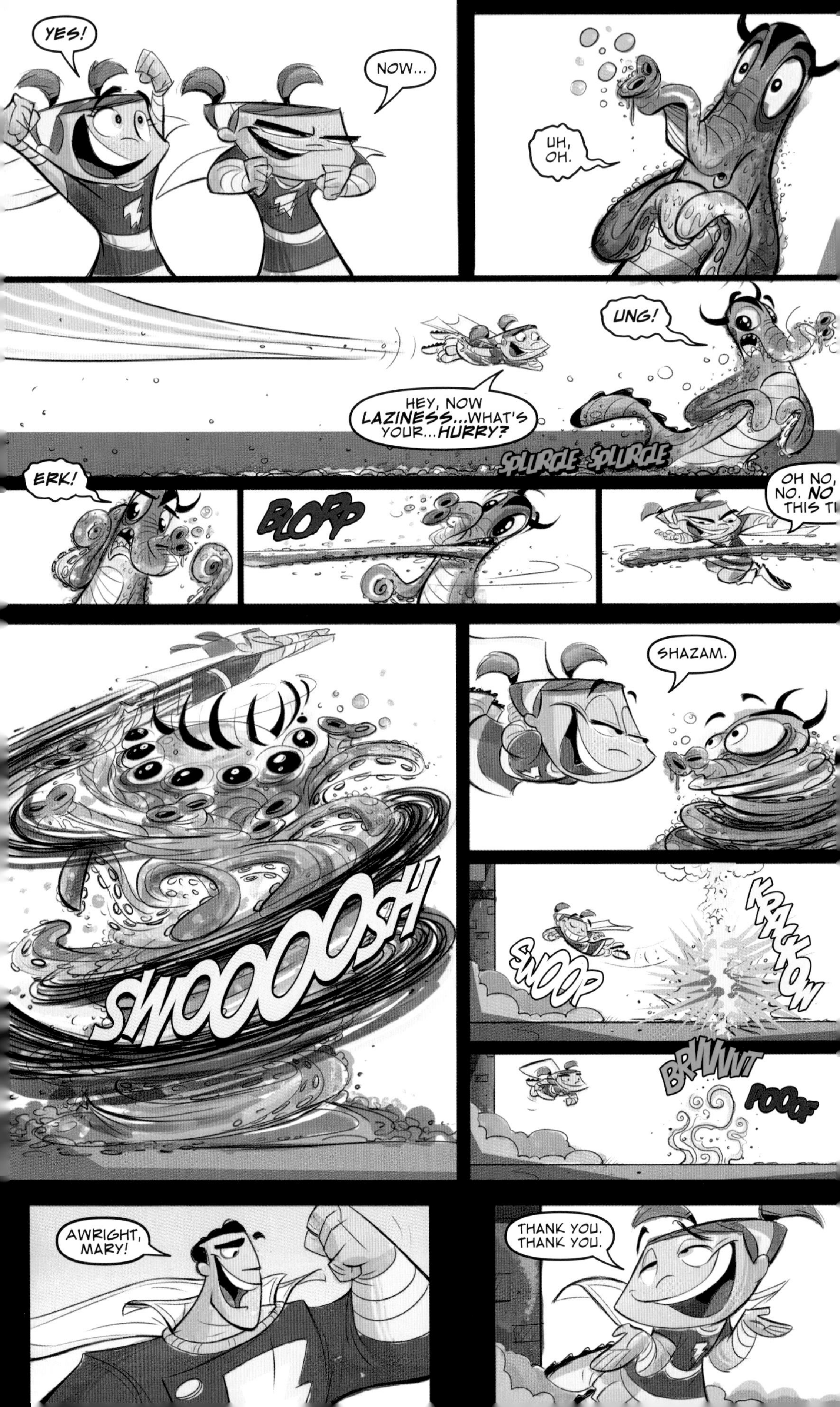
YES!
NOW...
UH, OH.
UNG!
HEY, NOW LAZINESS...WHAT'S YOUR...HURRY?
SPLURGLE SPLURGLE
ERK!
BLORP
OH NO, NO. NO
SWOOOOSH
SHAZAM.
SWOOP
KRACKOW
AWRIGHT, MARY!
THANK YOU. THANK YOU.

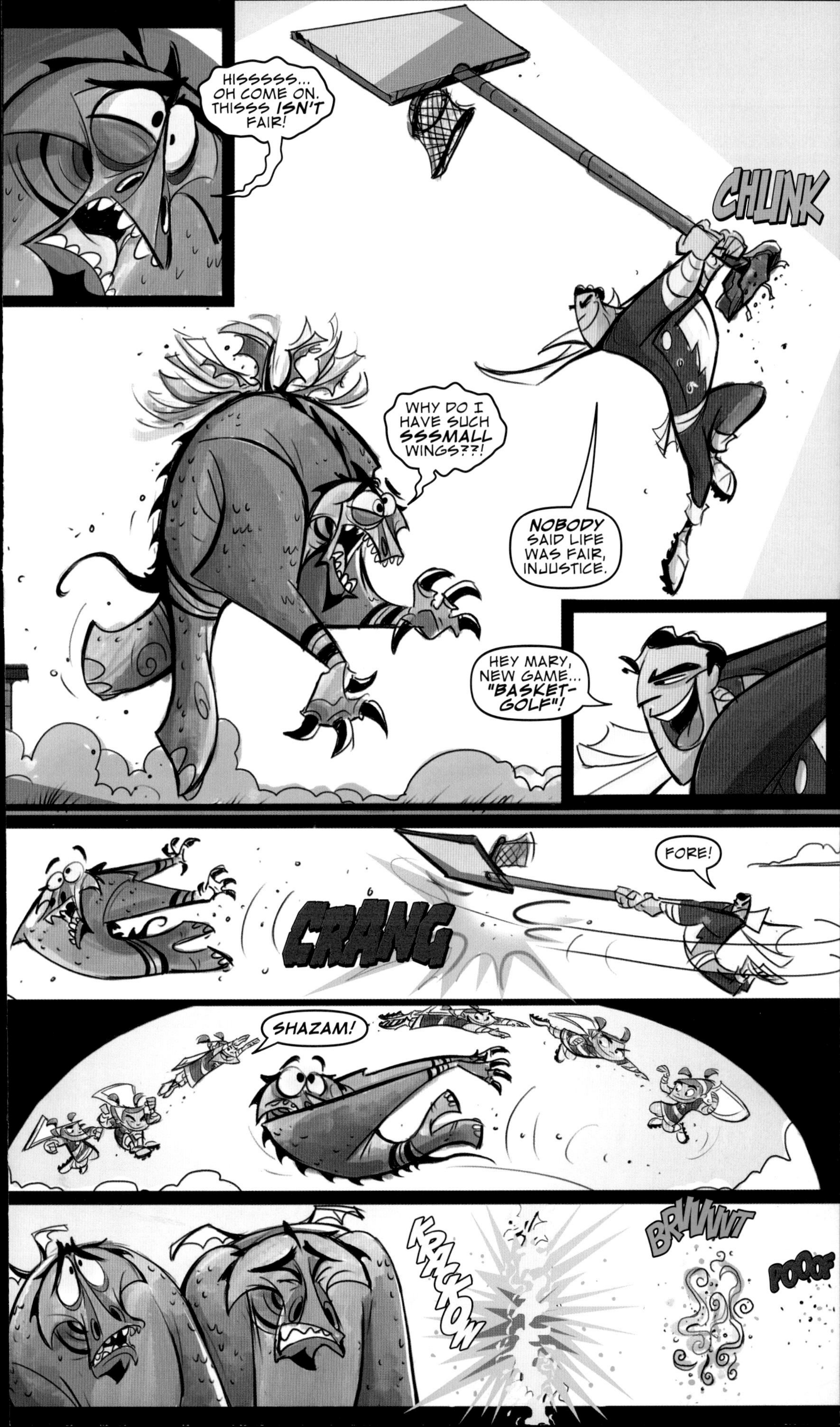

HISSSSS... OH COME ON. THISSS ISN'T FAIR!
CHUNK
WHY DO I HAVE SUCH SSSMALL WINGS??!
NOBODY SAID LIFE WAS FAIR, INJUSTICE.
HEY MARY, NEW GAME... "BASKET-GOLF"!
FORE!
CRANG
SHAZAM!
KRACKOW
BRVVVVVT
POOOF

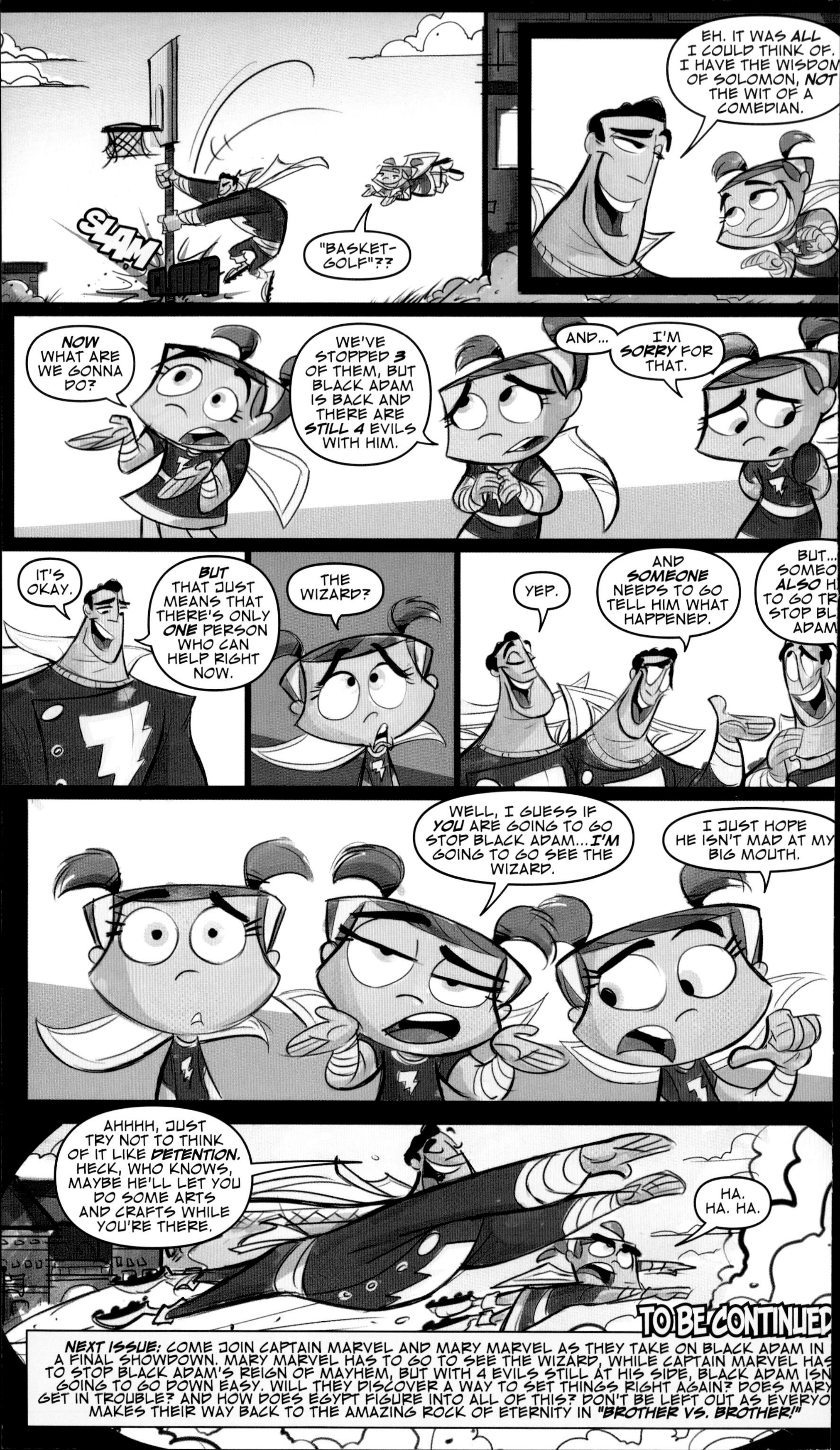
SLAM
CLANG
"BASKET-GOLF"??
EH. IT WAS ALL I COULD THINK OF. I HAVE THE WISDOM OF SOLOMON, NOT THE WIT OF A COMEDIAN.
NOW WHAT ARE WE GONNA DO?
WE'VE STOPPED 3 OF THEM, BUT BLACK ADAM IS BACK AND THERE ARE STILL 4 EVILS WITH HIM.
AND...
I'M SORRY FOR THAT.
IT'S OKAY.
BUT THAT JUST MEANS THAT THERE'S ONLY ONE PERSON WHO CAN HELP RIGHT NOW.
THE WIZARD?
YEP.
AND SOMEONE NEEDS TO GO TELL HIM WHAT HAPPENED.
BUT... SOMEO ALSO H TO GO TR STOP BL ADAM
WELL, I GUESS IF YOU ARE GOING TO GO STOP BLACK ADAM... I'M GOING TO GO SEE THE WIZARD.
I JUST HOPE HE ISN'T MAD AT MY BIG MOUTH.
AHHHH, JUST TRY NOT TO THINK OF IT LIKE DETENTION. HECK, WHO KNOWS, MAYBE HE'LL LET YOU DO SOME ARTS AND CRAFTS WHILE YOU'RE THERE.
HA. HA. HA.
TO BE CONTINUED
NEXT ISSUE: COME JOIN CAPTAIN MARVEL AND MARY MARVEL AS THEY TAKE ON BLACK ADAM IN A FINAL SHOWDOWN. MARY MARVEL HAS TO GO TO SEE THE WIZARD, WHILE CAPTAIN MARVEL HAS TO STOP BLACK ADAM'S REIGN OF MAYHEM, BUT WITH 4 EVILS STILL AT HIS SIDE, BLACK ADAM ISN GOING TO GO DOWN EASY. WILL THEY DISCOVER A WAY TO SET THINGS RIGHT AGAIN? DOES MARY GET IN TROUBLE? AND HOW DOES EGYPT FIGURE INTO ALL OF THIS? DON'T BE LEFT OUT AS EVERYO MAKES THEIR WAY BACK TO THE AMAZING ROCK OF ETERNITY IN "BROTHER VS. BROTHER!"

CREATOR

MIKE KUNKEL

When Mike Kunkel was a kid, he loved to write and draw stories. With over twenty years experience in the animation industry, Mike continues to do what he loves for a living. As a published writer and artist, Mike has been nominated three times for the prestigious Eisner Awards and four times for the Ignatz Awards. In fact, his original comic book series Herobear and the Kid won the Eisner Award--twice! Mike lives in Southern California where he spends most of his time drawing cartoons, learning new magic tricks, and playing with his family.

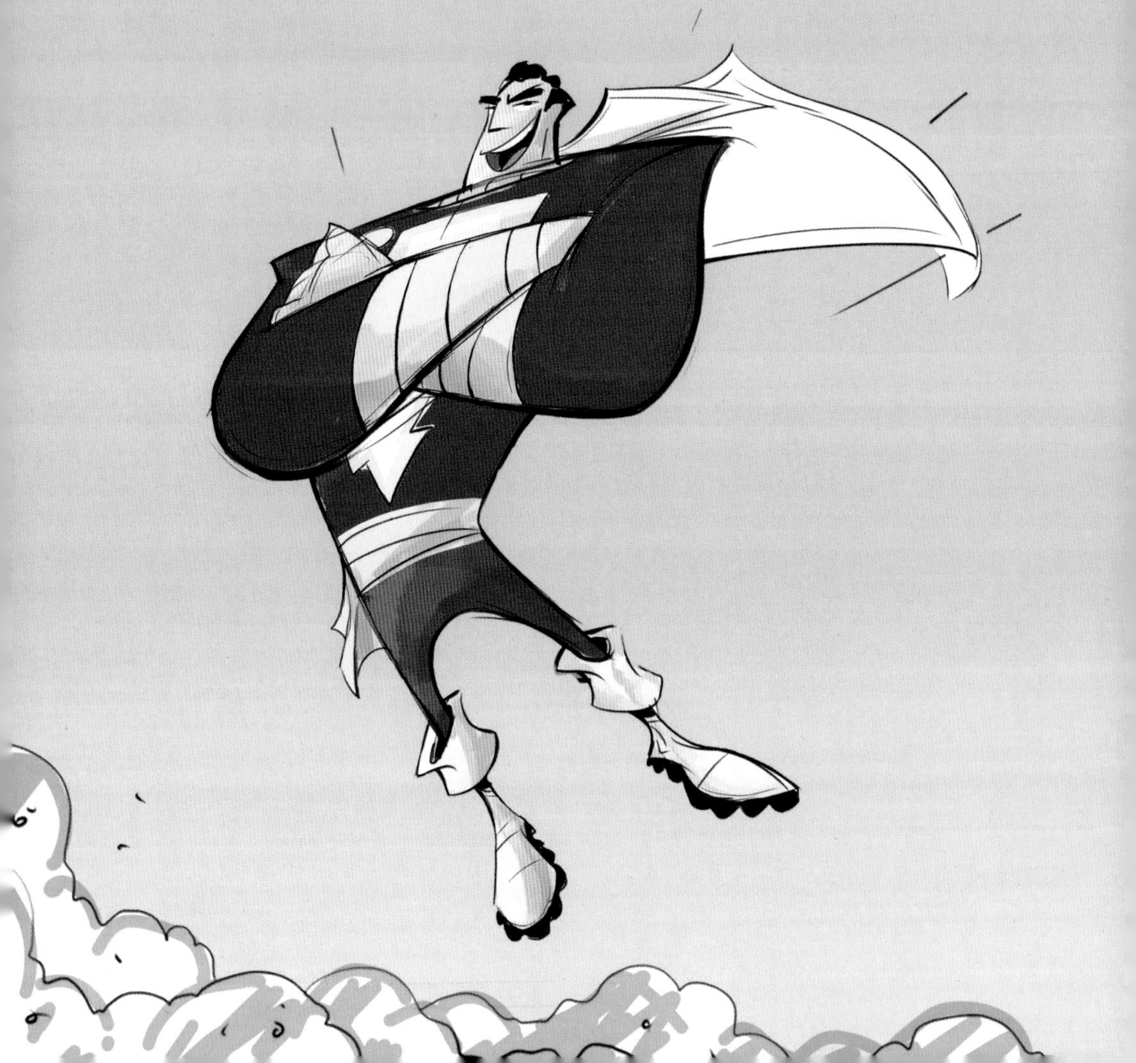

GLOSSARY

doom (DOOM)--unfortunate fate or destiny

fate (FATE)--a power beyond one's control that is believed to decide what happens

fulfilled (fuhl-FILLD)--accomplished or measured up to

mutant (MYOO-tuhnt)--something abnormal that has changed from a previous form

productive (pruh-DUK-tiv)--if something is productive, it gets results

protested (PRO-tess-tid)--objected strongly to, often in action as in a protest

puny (PYOO-nee)--weak or small or powerless

rebelled (ri-BELLD)--fought the authority or those in control

sloppy (SLOP-ee)--careless or messy

sustenance (SUHSS-tuh-nuhnss)--something that gives support, health, or strength

unfortunate (un-FOR-chuh-nit)--unlucky

wisdom (WIZ-dum)--learning acquired over a period of time

wit (WITT)--if you have wit, you are clever and think of smart things quickly

VISUAL QUESTIONS & PROMPTS

1. Which monster is Pride? How about Laziness? And what about Injustice? Explain your answers with clues from the monsters' appearances.

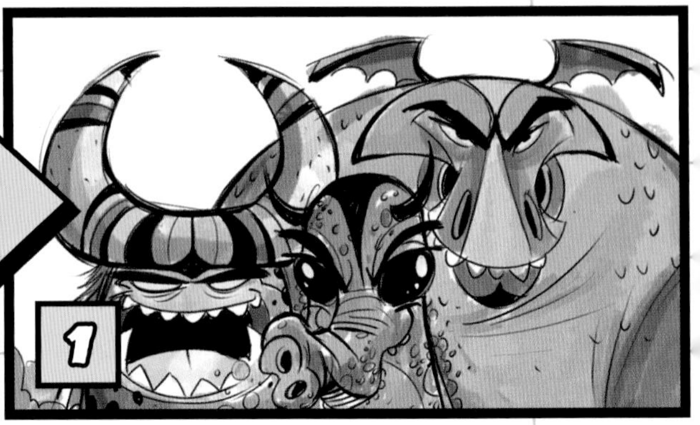
1

2. Why does Billy's speech bubble look different in this panel?

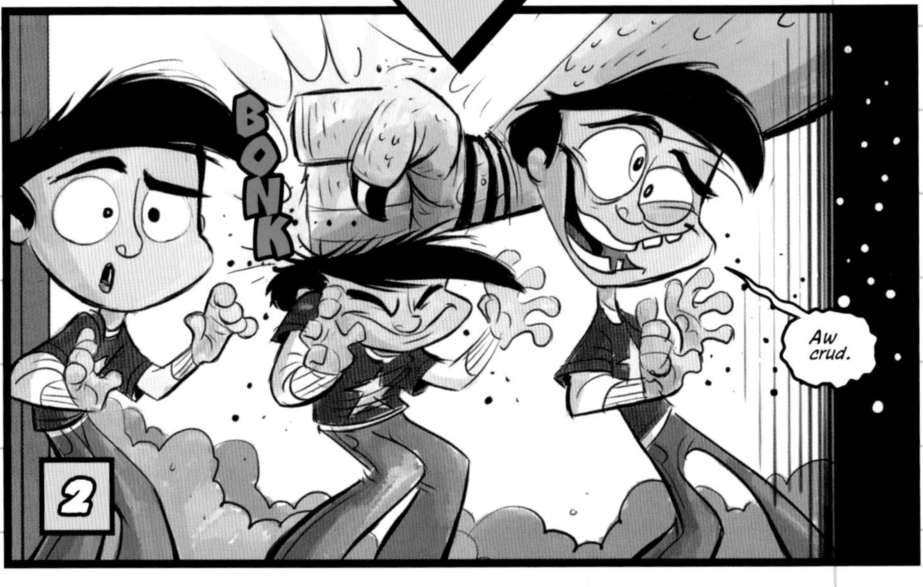
BONK
Aw crud.
2

3. Why do the four panels below look the way they do? What is happening here in this sequence of four illustrations?

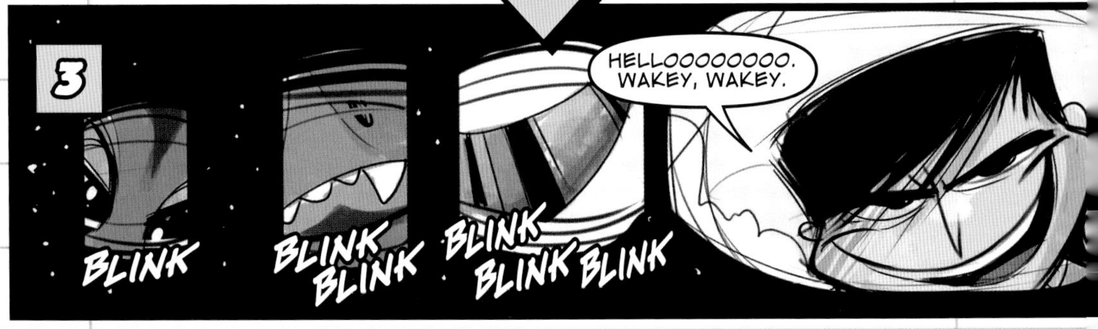
3
BLINK
BLINK BLINK
BLINK BLINK BLINK
HELLOOOOOOOO. WAKEY, WAKEY.

4. In this panel we see several events happening. Retell this panel with words instead of pictures, explaining the events of the panel step by step.

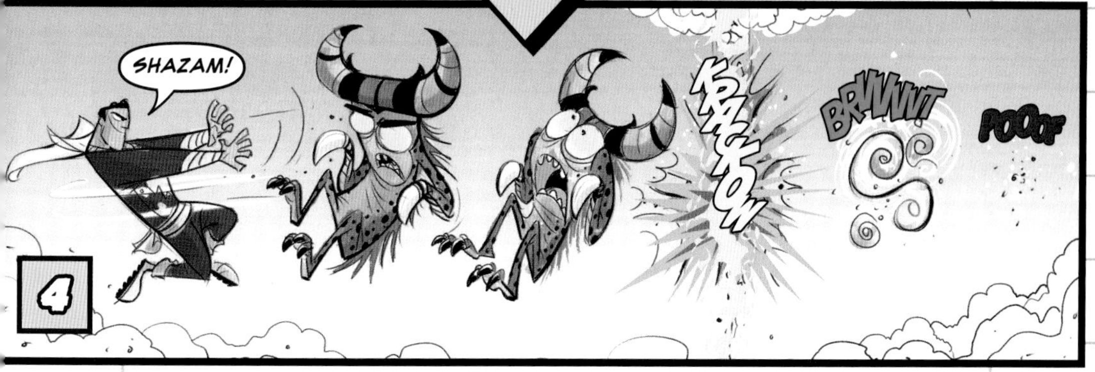
SHAZAM!
KRAKOW
BRVVVVVT
POOOF
4

5. If you could have any one of of the powers listed below, which one would you pick, and why?

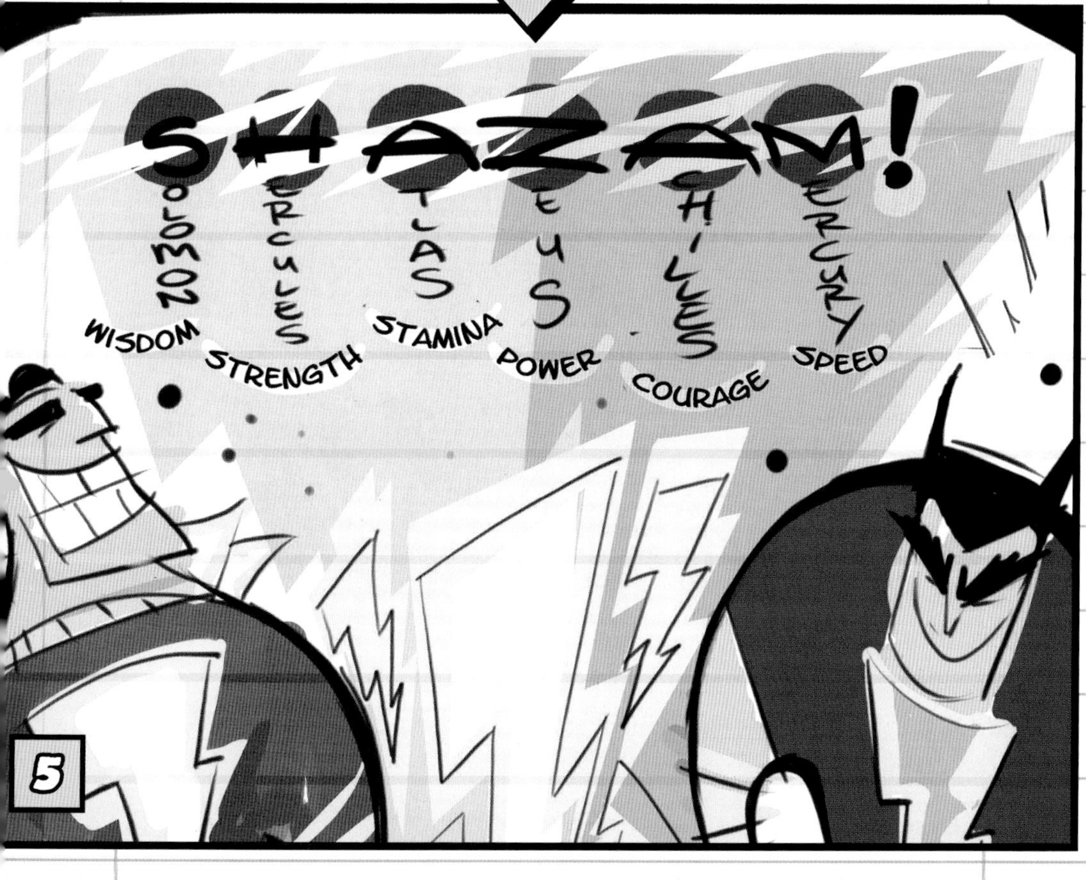
SHAZAM!
SOLOMON
HERCULES
ATLAS
ZEUS
ACHILLES
MERCURY
WISDOM
STRENGTH
STAMINA
POWER
COURAGE
SPEED
5

READ THEM ALL!

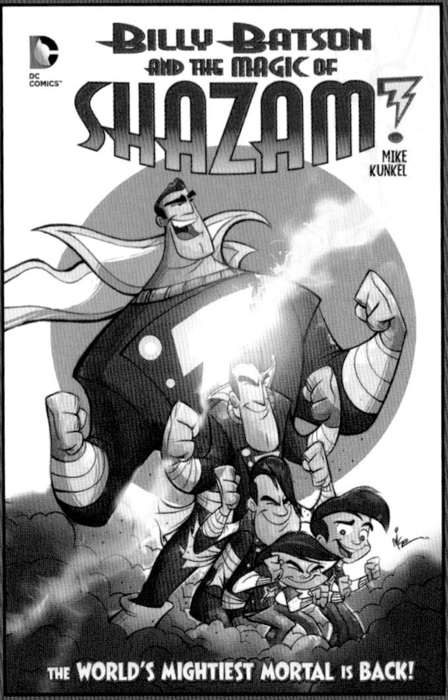
DC COMICS™
BILLY BATSON AND THE MAGIC OF SHAZAM!
MIKE KUNKEL
THE WORLD'S MIGHTIEST MORTAL IS BACK!

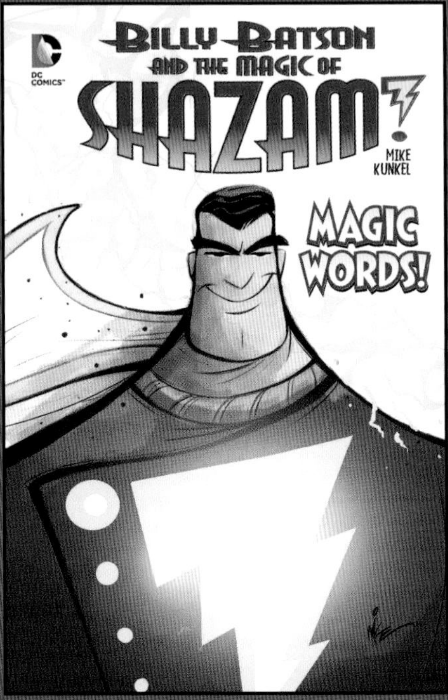
DC COMICS™
BILLY BATSON AND THE MAGIC OF SHAZAM!
MIKE KUNKEL
MAGIC WORDS!

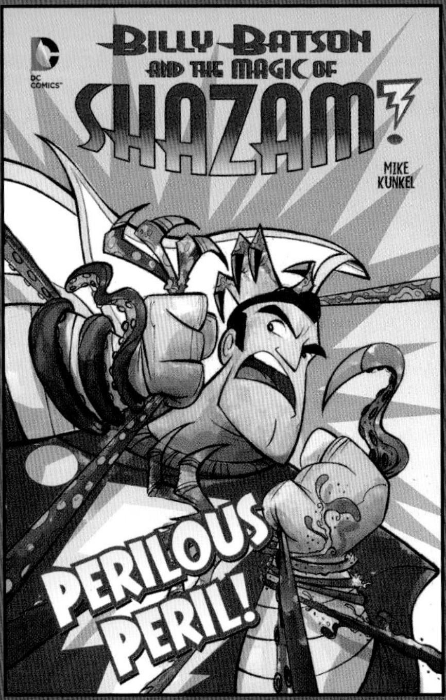
DC COMICS™
BILLY BATSON AND THE MAGIC OF SHAZAM!
MIKE KUNKEL
PERILOUS PERIL!

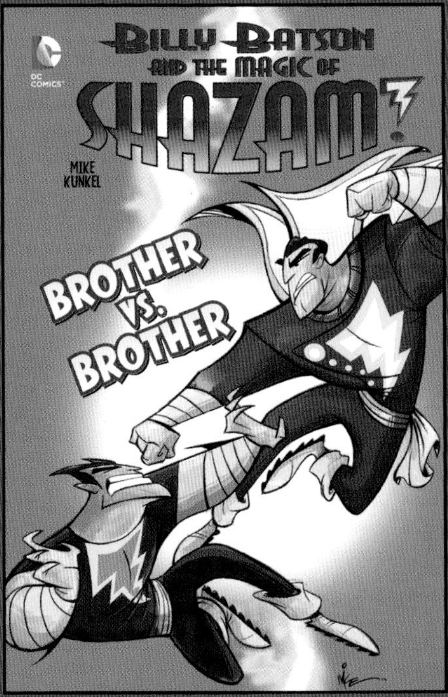
DC COMICS™
BILLY BATSON AND THE MAGIC OF SHAZAM!
MIKE KUNKEL
BROTHER VS. BROTHER

only from...

STONE ARCH BOOKS™